Among Animals

The Lives of Animals and Humans in Contemporary Short Fiction

Among Animals:

The Lives of Animals and Humans in

Contemporary Short Fiction

Edited by John Yunker

Published by Ashland Creek Press

www.ashlandcreekpress.com

ISBN 978-1-61822-025-7

Library of Congress Control Number: 2013944664

Contents

Introduction

As a society, we have a curious relationship with animals. Some animals we welcome into our homes and our lives. We tell them we love them. We call them our children. We become inconsolable when we lose them.

Other animals do not receive such adoration or protection. Some are viewed as nuisances, others as expendable. We keep our distance from these species. We use words like *anthropomorphize* so as not to get emotionally attached. We create mental hierarchies of animal intelligence so we may prioritize one species over another. We create barriers in our minds and on our lawns and in our legal systems to keep animals in their place and us in ours.

The stories in this anthology call attention to the many walls we have constructed.

At Ashland Creek Press, we believe that literature has an important role to play not only in reflecting the world around us but in changing it for the better. This anthology grew out of a desire to publish writing that re-examines and re-imagines our relationship with nature—specifically, with animals.

It's a relationship in need of serious therapy.

The short stories you will read here are as diverse as the species they depict, yet they also have much in common. Many of the stories underscore the equalities among humans and animals.

"Aren't You Pretty?" and "Beyond the Strandline" reveal that the grief and loss experienced as a result of injury and death are equal, regardless of species. And in "Litter," we experience firsthand the world through a stray dog's eyes.

In "Pelicans," we witness how an understanding of one species is vital to the survival of another. In "Greyhound," a rescued animal plays the role of rescuer. And in "The Weight of Things Unsaid," a baby turtle reminds a mother of two losses, human and animal, and the unbearable weight of each.

Some stories reveal that people who live on the edge of wilderness are often those most in conflict with it. In "Bad Berry Season," a park ranger does her best to keep bears and people apart, an increasingly futile effort with tragic and surprising consequences. In "Blue Murder," a farmer who is at odds with the local birds finds himself inexplicably drawn to an individual one.

The apparent contradictions between the animals we love and the animals we kill are not always so apparent to the characters of some stories. In "Emu," we watch the narrator tenderizing pork for dinner while praying for the sparing of a stray who showed up behind her home. In "Meat," a child's eyes shed light on the inconsistency of our society's yearning for "guilt-free" meat and the compassion we have for our pets.

And in "The Ecstatic Cry," a penguin researcher in Antarctica resists people, only to find that connections are similar in the animal and human worlds.

Sometimes, these connections emerge via the spiritual and mythological. In "The Boto's Child," a woman has an encounter with a mythical dolphin, and in "With Sheep," the lines between human and animal are blurred beyond distinction. In "Alas, Falada!" a zookeeper in mourning for an eland finds solace in a fairy tale.

"Miriam's Lantern," the last story in the anthology, deals with those who are last. In this haunting tale, a man must witness the extinction of a bird species, knowing that he played a role in its demise.

> *Day and night I brooded on letting the bird go. Together the two of us, of unrelated but closely connected species, from separate but closely related cages, would rise up into the sky—*

I hope you enjoy these stories as much as we have, and that you'll share them with others.

—John Yunker

Alas, Falada!

Diane Lefer

Humans get cremated. Animals just get burned. With a person, you do an autopsy to determine the cause of death. With an animal, we call it a *necropsy*, and in the eland's case, the distinction did make sense as we knew damn well what she died of. We had euthanized her ourselves. But she'd been sick a long time. If there was a microorganism spreading through the herd, we needed to know it, and so Ralphie drove her body out to the lab in San Bernardino. Then they sent me to bring back her head.

They told me to take one of the zoo trucks, but I'm not comfortable driving those things, so I went in my car. I assumed they would have the head packed on dry ice. They assumed I was bringing a container. They said they'd find a bag.

"Something opaque, please," I said, "and big." An eland is a *large* antelope.

A thirty-three-gallon garbage bag was the best they could do, and I put it on the front seat next to me, her two-foot-long horns sticking out. Not those massive heavy spirals, at least; she was a female.

It wasn't easy getting her to the car. An eland's horns go straight back, so I couldn't carry her facing away from me. Sideways would have worked, but I wasn't thinking all that clearly. As I carried her head in my arms, the plastic slipped, and I saw her face. Her eyes, gone flat and dry now, looked right at me.

Once I had her on the seat, I touched her—her once-soft nose all icy, a charcoal black smudge at the bridge. They must have burned the rest of her body. No one said.

The head was frozen solid, and, unless I hit traffic, was intended to stay that way the sixty-five miles to the Natural History Museum.

This was a good example of civic partnership and cooperation—cooperation being something I believe humans are genetically programmed for. Followers of Robert Ardrey (*African Genesis*, 1961)—not that we have anyone like that working here—would argue that no, our hardwiring is for aggression. A cynic might point out that we cooperate most selflessly and enthusiastically when the purpose *is* aggression, and I can't say I disagree. In any event, the museum was getting the head for its domestic beetle colony.

We are now in the midst of the Sixth Great Extinction, and while too many species are on the verge of disappearing altogether, it seems a new beetle is discovered almost every day. I understand if you're a major enough donor, the museum may name a new beetle species after you. I don't know how much you have to pay to put your name on a bug. I do know that it will cost you about $2,000 in "trophy fees" (plus travel, accommodations, meals, guides, and gratuities) if you kill or wound an eland in South Africa in order to bring the head home. A bargain compared to a white rhino head, which will run you about $30,000.

Once the beetles eat away the hair and flesh, we get the skull back for the education hall. I've never understood why we show children animal skulls so that they can no longer look on living creatures without thinking of death. All the same, and even though there's someone at the museum I really don't want to see, at first I thought our arrangement was a very good idea. The eland's end would come about much as though she'd died a natural death on the African plains, where she would have been returned to the soil as bacteria worked their decay and beetles, hyenas, and scavenger birds purified her right down to bone.

Ralphie, the vet tech, set me straight: "What? You think it's like a natural habitat where these bugs swarm over her head and pick it clean?" He told me the museum's beetles live half a dozen together in file drawers.

"Her head isn't going to fit in a file drawer," I said.

"Of course not. It has to be flensed."

Flense turned out to mean the hair and skin would be disposed of, though Ralphie declined to say how, and the flesh sliced up and dried. Then a slice would be left in each drawer. The beetles eat very slowly, inefficiently, Ralphie said, and it seemed to me if someone was going to devour you, you would hope at the very least it would be with gusto, with a very great hunger.

Even before I got in my car to go to San Bernardino, when I thought about it—hundreds of file drawers with tiny little beetles working their way without interest through her dried flesh—I had decided: No way could I be a party to this.

◈

Sometimes we do the necropsies on-site. I don't know what the determining factor is when we send them out. Much of what happens at the zoo is on a need-to-know basis, and we seem to be moving toward greater and greater secrecy.

The matter of names, for example. I used to know every animal by name, and not just from the ID number in the stud book. But people talk and word starts getting out and you have members of the public waving their arms and crying out "Caesar!" or "Inti!"—confusing these creatures who've learned to come when the keeper calls. Actually, we're not even sure which species and which individuals recognize the human speech sounds we've assigned them, but better to err on the side of caution.

The "someone" I didn't want to run into at the museum, by the way, is named Jamal. He is—or was—a juvenile chimpanzee. When he hanged himself—by accident, it is presumed, since though we do share almost 100 percent of our DNA, no one I know of has detected in the chimpanzee any tendency toward suicide—his body was so young and healthy and unmarred that rather than feed him to the beetles, it was decided to have him preserved and placed in an exhibit hall where he now delights schoolchildren by swinging on a vine just above their heads. They say he's very lifelike, but I knew *him*, his vitality, playfulness, and how just plain stubborn he could be. The thought of walking in and seeing Jamal stuffed? I couldn't bear it.

I don't believe he committed suicide, but I do know animals get sad. Many of us believe they—at least some of them—have consciousness, a range of emotions equal to humans, and a capacity for rational thought, while to others—the Ardrey-types I too often find married to my friends—this is heresy.

My office is decorated with paw prints on textured paper, handsomely framed. (Sometimes when an animal—lion or bear—is unconscious in the O.R., we take liberties.) More to the point are the abstract paintings done by JimBob the elephant and an orangutan named Colette. The compositions are so pleasing and the colors so harmonious to the eye, you cannot convince me the artists were not taking pleasure in what they were creating, that they were not operating out of a true aesthetic sense. When Majikan was here in recovery, he liked to look at pictures in magazines. It was clear some pleased him more than others, and while his taste and mine don't necessarily coincide, his show of preference surely proves he had his own criteria for passing judgment.

If an orangutan can think in aesthetic terms, a human should be able to, so you'll have to agree that the eland's still beautiful head deserved better than to be flensed. If you argue, instead, that Beauty earns its bearer no special dispensation, I—who am not myself beautiful—will argue back that *aesthetic* is the opposite of *anaesthetic*. It's the awakening of feeling, a welcome stimulus these days to heart and mind.

◈

No story bores me more than one that begins "When I was a child … " This is true even when I'm talking to myself, which I am in fact doing right now. The preceding argument about aesthetics has been raging—albeit in quiet and civilized fashion—inside my own head. Scientists say—though I'm not convinced—only humans can do this: project a mental image of ourselves and regard it. Use our imagination to explore choices without immediately suffering the consequence.

There is a frozen head slowly but surely beginning to defrost in front of my television set, large enough to block the screen, huge enough in import to block most other thoughts. I should have used my imagination before I brought this thing home. Now I have to decide what the hell I'm going to do with it. It is not offering me a solution although I somehow absurdly thought it would. The dread words sneak up on me: *When I was a child …*

When I was a child, like most children, I suspect, I believed animals could talk. I saw no separation between them and me. I wanted a pet zebra I could ride bareback and a monkey smart enough to beat me at gin rummy, and when asked what I wanted to be when I grew up, I thought the choice was open enough that I always answered, "A sea otter." Other children wanted to be tigers, eagles. I had no dreams of power or imperial might.

"You wanted to be cute," Ralphie has said to me, but I was never thinking *cute*. Sea otters looked happy.

My favorite Grimm fairy tale was "The Goose-Girl," in which the severed head of the betrayed princess's slaughtered horse is nailed on the dark gateway to the city. Whenever she passes it while tending the geese, she cries, "Alas, Falada, hanging there!" and the head answers her. As I drove back from San Bernardino, I spoke to the eland's head in the trash bag beside me, and I called her "Falada."

In the story, Falada, the horse, spoke intelligible German even before he (or she) was killed, but it must have been the lingering effect of that story that made me feel now, as an adult, when I no longer expect to share a spoken language with the zebras and the seals, that Falada's head in the passenger seat, mute in life, had something to say, and I would surely hear it if I could only divine the right way to listen.

Surely there was a message. I pulled over and put her head in the trunk.

◈

I was there when Falada died. My job title is administrative assistant, but we're shorthanded—budget cuts—and sometimes I get called to the waiting room to keep a frightened animal company until the vet is free. Sometimes

I get to watch surgery through the window, and sometimes I'm even called to the O.R. to stroke an animal in distress. My favorite vet is Ginger. They're all great. They come in on their days off, forego their vacations, come in early and stay late—they have to because we only have two, plus one part-time—and they do it willingly because they love the animals. But it was Ginger who, when we had the tiger in quarantine, said, "I never wanted to have babies, but if I could give birth to a tiger cub, I'd do it in a minute."

"So would I," I said, "if you could guarantee it would only take a minute." I made it a joke even though I was profoundly moved.

◆

Falada was so old and weak, she could hardly walk anymore or hold herself up on her feet. They'd already knocked her down with tranqs before they loaded her into the truck and brought her to us from the barn. She'd lost so much weight her skin was loose on her shrunken frame, and Ginger, Ralphie, and I were able to get her to the O.R. by ourselves. We have a hydraulic lift to get animals onto the gurney, but when you're talking about something big—a camel, say—it still takes several men pushing to get the gurney to roll. Or women, if you had women strong enough, which none of us working here now happens to be.

Ginger set up the I.V. The three of us gathered around to say good-bye.

You have to understand that veterinary medicine, especially for zoo animals, is a very inexact science. In the old days, not so long ago, Ginger says if an animal got sick, you just called the nearest horse doctor for advice. Sometimes animals are still taken to specialists in human disease. There's a lot more research done on dogs and cats than on elands, so a lot of what happens at the zoo is based on trial and error, experience, seat-of-the-pants, which is maybe not so different from medical care for humans, except with humans you don't like to admit it.

Falada's hold on life was already so tenuous, it seemed it would take little to snuff it out, but drugs can have unpredictable effects. When muscles twitched beneath her coat, we assumed this was approaching death. But then, as though someone had turned on the switch for an animatronic figure, all at once, everything started up: lungs wheezing, white lips flapping, her thin legs drumming against the table, eyes flaring open and rolling, her whole body jerking like Frankenstein's monster, galvanized. Her head shook, dangerous with those horns, and we swarmed her body. We fastened straps and we held her down, with the *rat-a-tat-tat* of her drumming jolting, vibrating up my arms. It would have been more humane, I thought, to fire a bullet right into that light-colored chevron patch between her eyes. I could feel her heart racing and I could feel the impulse to run beating against her skin as Ginger prepared another syringe and Falada's dewlap trembled and slapped against me as she strained and my fingers twisted through the coarse fringe of hair. My cheek against her chestnut flank, I stroked along each white stripe and over the raw places where her coat was mangy and scabbed.

The eland was not an animal I knew well, but I lay against her body, selflessly, I like to think, with no concern for ticks or fleas as Ginger administered still another injection until the jerking and quivering and straining stopped.

When indigenous people kill an animal, they honor or propitiate it in some way, or so I've read, because only this will ensure that the animals will continue to thrive and allow man to kill them. When we euthanized Falada, we did it sadly, solemnly, without pleasure, to the best of our ability, with horror and with great regret, but we failed in the ritual that would ensure the multiplication and swarm of life.

When it was finally over, Ginger put her arms around me, which was a little scary because while I swear I'm not a lesbian, the truth is, if I were going to love someone—a human, that is—again, I really do think it would be Ginger.

◈

In "The Goose-Girl," the true status of the princess is revealed, and she marries the prince. Nothing more is said about the head of the ever-faithful horse—no mention of decent burial, or a magical restoration, or its reduction to bone. An oversight? I consider it injustice.

All of which may help explain, though not excuse, why instead of going to the museum when I left the lab, I drove back to the zoo.

"The museum must have sent someone," I said. "The head was already gone."

Then I finished my regular shift, hoping she hadn't yet thawed in my trunk.

The museum had Jamal. That was enough. I wasn't going to let them have Falada.

◈

Once I got her head home, I knew that sooner or later I'd be caught. Like any criminal—or most—I wasn't thinking about how I was going to get away with it. It didn't seem to matter. It was obvious I hadn't thought any of this through. She wouldn't fit in my freezer. You may be thinking: "So what? Go out and buy a full-size." But a person who commits a crime on impulse is not thinking coolly and logically. I certainly wasn't. The only reality that got through to me was this: I was in danger of losing the best job I ever had. Once, I did two years of social work, but having reached the conclusion that altogether too many humans are greedy, mean-spirited, and just plain stupid, I could no longer bring myself to make any efforts on their behalf. Now it's a privilege to be working alongside such good people who are doing so much good.

As I said the other day to Ginger, "When you save the life of a bear cub, you don't have to worry he'll go out and vote Republican."

◈

Ginger had tears in her eyes when Falada died.

I'm probably more of a pedophile than a lesbian since I'm only attracted to women, like her, who look like young boys. Slim hipped, flat on top, smooth hairless skin. I tell myself it's not sexual desire for a child but nostalgia for puppy love. They remind me of the first little boys I had crushes on, the little boys I wanted to kiss and marry and live with forever after. It's a desire for that innocence, the attachments that were fierce and fiercely ignorant of the world. The attachment I feel for the animals.

Which side are you on? Theirs, I think, *theirs*.

Do I bury her furtively at night? Leave her head in the open air beneath the great oak in Stough Park, where a woman once told me she'd been very satisfied so far with the Druid lifestyle? Will I end up tossing her from my speeding car on a stretch of the Angeles Crest Highway reputed to be a landfill for victims?

Tell me, I say. *Tell me what you want.*

I have comforted a frightened tamarin. Baboons have

masturbated in my direction with zestful glee. An anxious, white-cheeked gibbon once grasped my hand while her mate was being treated by Ginger. I'd held Falada throughout her last struggle. Even now, I can't say whether in those throes that didn't want to end she was struggling harder to live or to die. If I could shed my humanness, I would. But such transformation happens only in myths and fairy tales.

There were many variant stories collected by the Brothers Grimm. Mostly we know the child-friendly sanitized versions. Is there another tale in which Falada is acknowledged? In which the princess meets her death and the horse is restored to life? I have never found it. *Alas, Falada, hanging there!* You were the most vivid part of the story, the part I remember, and when it ends, with right triumphing over wrong, you are not only dead but forgotten, still forsaken.

She has tipped over onto my floor, and a puddle begins to spread past the plastic. In all her years of being looked at, I wonder how many people ever saw her as anything more than one of the herd. I think of how she strained so hard and rhythmically against the bonds that held her, her whole body like one big heart, beating, beating.

My own fight ends so quickly. What can I do but deliver you into those human hands? A private transaction. No exhibition hall, no public door. I knew this all along: There's a service entrance with a long slow ramp winding down into the dark. That's where we'll tread, you in my arms. I won't have to see Jamal. I won't have to look into your eyes, Falada.

Greyhound

Jean Ryan

This place is not like the pound—greyhounds don't bark, nor do they make any frenetic appeals for freedom, nor do their sleek bodies betray any sign of disease. Professional athletes, these dogs have been fed and watered with precision. Now, finally pardoned, they rest comfortably in their cages, and as I approach, they raise their heads and eye me warily: What am I doing here? What do I want from them?

Pick one, I keep telling myself. But how? They look away, refuse to help me.

"Do you know anything about them?" I ask the attendant, a plump blonde in a tight green uniform. "Their personalities, I mean."

"Sure." She pushes herself off the wall and points to the dog in front of us. "That's Digger Dan. He's five. Raced in eight states. He's stubborn but real smart. And that's Buck Shot. He's four, kind of skittery."

We move down the row. "Shoot the Moon's a good dog." She shrugs. "They're all good dogs." We stop at another cage and peer at a brindled greyhound the colors of a fawn. "This one's new." The blonde puts her hands on her hips and chuckles. "You know what she did? She stopped running. The gate opened one day, and she wouldn't budge."

She is lying still as a sphinx, paws neatly crossed, tail tucked away. Her deep brown eyes appraise us; there's no telling what she concludes. I stare back, and her gaze slides off.

"How old is she?" I ask.

"Three. She ran for just over a year. Clara's Gift, they called her. She was good, a favorite. Funny the way she quit."

The dog is waiting for us to leave—I can see the tension in the sculpted muscles of her back.

I wonder if, tired of racing, she planned her defection. How long did it take her to get up the nerve? Did she know when they led her to the track that day?

Or maybe the idea came to her suddenly. Maybe, as she crouched behind the gate, as the crowd filled the bleachers, she added the whole thing up and saw at long last that she was being duped: The rabbit wasn't real.

"Can I pet her?" I ask.

"They're not used to affection," the blonde says, opening the cage. "They don't understand it."

I come closer, and the dog rises to a sitting position. Her eyes are large and apprehensive. Carefully I extend my hand; she sniffs it and shrinks. When I touch her, she flinches. "Good girl," I soothe, and though she allows me to pet her shoulder, it's not much fun for either of us.

Great. I could have gone to the pound and come back thirty minutes later with a fat, tail-wagging puppy, but here I am at the greyhound shelter, 112 miles from home, offering up my heart to a dog who just wishes I'd go away.

I arch an eyebrow at the attendant, and she smiles sympathetically. "They're all like that in the beginning," she assures me, "and then, after a few weeks, they can't get enough of it." Dubious, I turn back to the dog, who is looking at my arm as if it were a rolled-up newspaper.

"Just move slowly," she says. "They don't like sudden movements. And they don't like having their crate space invaded."

"Crate space?"

She nods. "Greyhounds spend most of their time in crates—they sleep in them; they feel safe in them. These cages are like their crates."

I pull my arm out, and the dog cautiously lowers herself back down. There is no waste on this animal; she is muscle and tendon, angle and bone; even her veins have no place to hide. Her forelegs are so thin and straight I have to turn away. There must be thirty dogs here, all posed in their cages, remote and silent as statuary.

"I thought they'd be old," I say.

"Oh no. Two years of racing is about the norm. Some of them run longer—you can tell by their paws." She points to a large black-and-white hound. "Like that one. See how his front toes are twisted? The oval track does that. Most of these dogs are retired because of injury, or because they stop winning."

"Or running," I add, bringing my gaze back to Clara's Gift, realizing I have made my choice. And she knows, too, even before I tell the attendant. Alarmed, she gets to her feet, prepares to submit. It breaks my heart how good she is about being taken away, how dignified her walk to my truck. What price has she paid to behave like that?

Figuring she might enjoy some scenery for a change, I let her ride in the cab. She perches on the bench seat, taking up almost no space, and looks worriedly out the window. I keep murmuring assurances, but my voice doesn't calm her. As soon as we merge onto the highway and the Oregon mountains begin rushing by, she crawls off the seat and into the back of the cab.

◈

The dog is a present for Holly, a surprise. She thinks I'm running errands for the store, picking up organic lettuces and local honey. That's where we met, my health food store. She came in one day and showed me the patches of eczema on her arms and asked me what she could do about them. I told her she might try using a humidifier, and I sold her some B-complex vitamins and a bar of oatmeal soap. Not long after that she moved in with me, and six years later we're still together, and still battling that eczema.

Not every day, of course—it comes and goes like magic. For weeks, even months, her limbs are as smooth and pale as the creamy hollows of a seashell. Most of the bouts are mild—mainly on her arms and the back of her hands—but there are times when the rash terrifies us both, when it moves up her neck and down her chest, turning the skin into a silvery crust, till she hides herself even from me. Those are the times she can't sleep, and I find her on the back steps rocking herself in the moonlight.

This has been a tough year for Holly—four episodes already—and two weeks ago, at the start of another flare-up, she quit her job at the Talking Turtle Day Care Center. The parents were making comments, she told me. "They get edgy at the sight of a rash, especially on an adult."

"What about the children?" I asked. "What do they say?"

"Oh, they don't mind. They just want to know if it hurts."

I have persuaded her to take at least six months off, hoping some private time will hush her demons (of course I don't mention this, for fear of jinxing her). I must admit I like the idea of her at home, making cheese lasagna and repotting plants. Still, it's a shame about the day care center: Nobody's better with children than Holly. She can remember their world, can still lose herself gazing at a puddle of tadpoles. She is childlike even in appearance, with her thin limbs and small, sharp features. People can't believe she is thirty-nine years old.

A dog, I thought, would be a good idea, would satisfy Holly's nurturing needs while presenting fewer challenges than a roomful of children bored with their toys. So when I saw the ad for adopting a retired greyhound, I couldn't ignore the serendipity.

◈

Now, halfway home, glancing at the pile of literature they gave me, I'm having second thoughts. Greyhounds come with a list of warnings: Did I know they shouldn't be left alone? Is my neighborhood quiet? Any toddlers in the house? And is there a fenced-in field nearby? Once these dogs start running, God knows where they'll end up.

All I can see of Clara's Gift are her front paws; she hasn't moved in more than an hour, hasn't offered so much as a sigh. I don't expect her to jump around joyfully, but why, on the other hand, doesn't she whimper? For all she knows, we could be heading for another racetrack.

I think of her sticklike limbs; they remind me of invalids, of nursing homes and wheelchairs. Suddenly I don't think I can do this. I am a large woman, big-boned—you wouldn't guess, looking at Holly and me, that I'm the squeamish one. Truth is, I can't stomach the suffering of animals; I can't even walk into a pet store. An exit sign appears, and I move into the right lane. Would it be so unforgivable, bringing back this damaged dog?

But I don't. I take her home to Holly, as I do the fallen fledglings I find, and all the other hapless creatures I don't know how to fix.

◆

"She needs a special diet. And we have to walk her twice a day." I'm citing the drawbacks right away, letting Holly know what we're up against. "And, ah, she isn't housebroken either—none of them are."

But Holly is scarcely listening. Sitting on her heels, facing the dog, she is already smitten.

"She's so delicate," Holly says. "Like a deer, or like one of those tiny primeval horses."

"We'll have to run her in the soccer field, a couple times a week," I add. "Greyhounds need to run."

"What did you say they called her?"

"Clara's Gift."

"What kind of a name is that?" Holly shakes her head. "No. We'll call her"—she pauses, smiles—"we'll call her Fawn." At the utterance of this word, soft and perfect, the dog lifts her small folded ears.

◆

Shortly after arriving, Fawn wedges herself behind the sofa. "The room is too big," I explain to Holly. We find a cardboard carton in the garage, and Holly covers the bottom of it with an afghan her mother crocheted. We place the box next to the sofa, and, quick as a card trick, Fawn is inside.

◆

For the next few days, Fawn spends most of her time in that makeshift crate, calmly watching us drink our coffee, read the mail, open and close the drapes. At night though, when Holly and I are in bed, I sometimes see her dark silhouette in the doorway. "Come here, Fawn," I coax, "come here, girl." But she declines the invitation, and after a while I hear her nails clicking down the hall as she makes her way back to her box. Whatever she needs, it's not our company.

As far as upkeep, she's no trouble at all. In fact, she's already housebroken. All I did was lay down some newspaper in a corner, and each morning I moved the papers a little closer to the back porch, and by the third day she was waiting at the door. There is something uncanny about this dog, some kind of age-old wisdom behind those luminous eyes. I get the feeling she is smarter than me and obeys out of politeness. Not that I need to issue many commands; Fawn comports herself so flawlessly I am embarrassed to put her on a leash. They told me to hold her firmly, that the twitch of a squirrel's tail would make her bolt. Well, we've seen plenty of squirrels, and even a few jackrabbits zigzagging through the scrub oak, and Fawn ignores them all. We've tried everything, from throwing sticks and Frisbees to jogging way ahead of her, and the thing is, she just won't run.

◈

I am sitting on the sofa studying vitamin catalogs. Holly is lying on the carpet next to Fawn; over and over, her hand moves down the smooth slope of the dog's neck. Fawn no longer needs the box, and while she doesn't exactly ask for affection, she doesn't object to it either (unless you try to hug her—she can't bear that).

I spend too much time on these catalogs. They used to be newsprint pamphlets; today they're slick with photos, hefty as phonebooks. When I opened Earthly Goods eighteen years ago, there wasn't a pill in the place, just brown rice and bulgur and some bug-ravaged produce. I liked it that way; I liked the weirdly shaped tomatoes and the warm hayloft smell when I opened the door each morning. Now I'm buying amino wafers and colloidal silver, royal jelly and blue-green algae. I had to cut back on the produce to make room for the bodybuilding products. Half of the back wall is devoted to nothing but B vitamins. I want to reduce my inventory, but everything sells: grape-seed extract, lutein, selenium, milk thistle, bovine cartilage. People are frantic for elixirs, and I'm the town supplier. I'm not even culpable when the potions don't work: The fault could lie in the alignment of the stars, in the user's lack of faith. That's the key to this booming business—the disclaimer's built right in.

I push aside the catalogs and consider the raw patches of skin on Holly's arms. Certainly nothing on my shelves has worked any miracles here. I wonder why the rash is so persistent this time and how bad it will get. Holly claims she has no secrets, no private well of grief: I can't believe this. I want to ask all the old questions, one by one, to see if there's something we've missed.

"Such soft fur," Holly says, her hand moving slowly, reverently down the dog's back. "They used to have wiry coats, like Airedales, but that's been bred out of them." Holly has been reading everything she can find on the subject of greyhounds. "Their eyes weren't this big either—the breeders decided that big eyes would make them see the lure better, so they elongated the head and made the occipital cavities larger—the sense of smell was impaired in the process, but nobody cared about that."

She sighs. "They even changed the tails, made them longer so they could work like rudders. The only trouble is, they keep breaking. Puppies break their tails all the time. Their legs break too, especially the Italian greyhounds."

I think of the times I've seen Fawn gingerly lick her legs, or stare at them in a kind of bewilderment. At first we thought she might be in pain, which would explain her reluctance to run, but the vet said no, she was fine. "She's still a young dog," he said. "You really should run her—otherwise she'll get fat and then she really will have problems."

Fawn's gaze is fixed on the carpet. Greyhounds originated in Egypt, Holly told me, and were called "gazehounds." I observe Fawn's glistening brown eyes, their dark depths keeping the secrets of the pharaohs. How can we make it up to her? How can we explain this powder-blue carpet to an animal that once roamed the banks of the Nile?

"I've never seen her wag her tail," I say. "Have you?"

"No," Holly says softly. She raises her hand and cups the small blameless dome of Fawn's head; the dog responds with a look of forbearance in which I can glimpse the burgeoning of devotion.

"Fawn has never been alone," Holly says. "She's lived her whole life with other dogs. Maybe we should let her spend some time with Maxine and Crash."

We share a nervous glance. Maxine and Crash live next door. Maxine is an old, one-eyed mastiff; overweight, hobbled by arthritis, she still hauls herself over to the fence at the slightest provocation. Crash is a two-year-old black lab who in endless ebullience hurls his body into whatever objects lie in his path. Neither one is very bright, and they both bark too much, a habit we don't want Fawn to pick up.

"We could try it," Holly says. "We could take her over there and see how it goes."

I am weighing alternatives. There is a Chihuahua down the road who can teach Fawn nothing I want her to learn. Frank and Dora's Dalmatian would be more suitable, but they live four miles away; we'd have to drive there every time, and I really don't like Frank.

"Okay," I finally answer.

Fawn is studying the carpet again. I am sending my autistic child off to public school.

◈

We have two rocks in our living room, boulders really; Holly rolled them in from the woods. There is a cavity in one, which she keeps filled with water; she's planted some emerald moss around it and a few tiny ferns. Miniature worlds—that's her fetish. Right now, she's working on a desert scene: a shallow clay bowl filled with sand to which she has introduced some baby cacti, a twig painted like a snake, an Ivory soap steer skull the size of a cough drop, and a prospector's shack she fashioned out of splinters from our fence. Last night she was talking about turning the hallway into a prehistoric diorama.

Holly went to art school back east and after graduation found herself on Fifth Avenue designing window displays. The winter scenes were the most fun, she said: the pumpkins and fall leaves, the sparkling drifts of plastic snow. Still, she got tired of the gaunt mannequins and the New York winters, and the next thing she knew she was in San Francisco, creating curb appeal not for clothing stores but for small restaurants. She was very successful at this, and I wonder if she ever resents the urge that brought her to Agness, Oregon. While Holly has no trouble telling me about the mating rituals of the trumpeter swan or the ramifications of the greenhouse effect, she rarely imparts information about herself; most of what I know about her I've had to piece together. If she has fallen short of her goals, if she yearns for something more than me and this house we're constantly mending, she doesn't burden me with it.

◈

We are taking Fawn over to Will and Theda's, the owners of Maxine and Crash. Will and Theda built their house out of aluminum cans and plastic jugs and God knows what else. In their backyard is an old washing machine they use as a smoker; in a gutted refrigerator next to it, they raise crayfish. There is always a chicken or two strutting around and several cats, and though I love Will and Theda, I'm getting more and more uneasy at the idea of exposing Fawn to their country chaos.

As usual, Theda is up to her elbows in flour—she bakes pies and cookies for a bakery in town—and Will is out back working on the tractor. For devotees of the simple life, they're the busiest people I know.

"How's our sweet baby girl?" Theda coos, reaching for Fawn with floured hands. Fawn ducks, backs up.

"She's nervous," I apologize. "New surroundings."

"Well, of course she is," Theda says. She settles her hands on her wide hips and beams at Fawn. "She's such a pretty little thing!"

Fawn cranes her neck, taking everything in. Back hunched, tail tight between her legs, she is standing on the linoleum as if she were poised on a flat of eggs.

We have already discussed Fawn's problem with Theda, and she was more than happy to offer her dogs as a course of treatment. "Dogs need dogs," she said, "like people need people." In no time at all, she assured us, Fawn would be running like the wind.

"Are you ready, little one?" she says, grinning, and Fawn looks up at Holly for an answer.

We follow Theda's thick blonde braid and swaying hips out of the house; sure enough, there's a pair of orange chickens pecking up dust near the back steps. "Hold her tight," I whisper to Holly—just in case. The chickens stop feeding; each aims an eye at Fawn, who is trying to slink by without any trouble. Theda stamps her Birkenstock, and they scrabble away. On the other side of the steps, a black cat is lounging in a cracked flowerpot. As we walk past, she stops washing her paw and turns her cool green gaze on Fawn; almost immediately she loses interest and resumes her bath.

"Hey!" Will calls. We look to the left and see him waving from atop the tractor. Will is tall and rail-thin; with his long hair and straggly beard, he reminds me of Jesus. Crash is running circles around the tractor and barking frantically.

"Crash!" Theda yells. The dog stops, turns his head. "Here, Crash!"

Now he is racing toward us, full tilt, flat out. Fawn, seeing what's coming, freezes; Holly crouches down next to her. Theda chuckles and, stepping forward, grabs Crash's collar just before he slams into us.

"Stay," she orders, holding him back; he shivers, whines, tries to squirm forward. "Lie *down*."

This last command has some effect. Tongue lolling, sides heaving, Crash glances up at Theda, then back at Fawn, and, giving up, lowers his belly to the dirt. Fawn, meanwhile, hasn't moved; her ears are flattened to her skull.

"I'll let him go in a minute," Theda says. "He'll be fine." Slowly Holly gets to her feet. With her free hand, Theda ruffles the fur on Crash's neck. "Beast," she declares, and gives us a wink.

When Theda finally lets go of Crash, he shoots over to Fawn and starts sniffing. She doesn't try to flee, she doesn't growl—she just sinks to the ground and stays there, and while his tail swings near her head and his wet nose quivers over her haunches, she looks the other way. She pretends he isn't there.

For the next hour and a half, Fawn doesn't move, not even when Maxine lumbers over and flops down beside her. Next to Fawn, Maxine is more hideous than ever with that enormous square head and white puckered eye and those gums hanging out of her mouth. Will gives up on the tractor, and the four of us sit on the back steps drinking homemade beer and watching Crash wear himself out: He whimpers at Fawn, he jogs back and forth, he falls on his front legs and barks in her face. But she gives him only an occasional baffled glance, and at last he collapses at our feet.

Theda shrugs. "We'll try again tomorrow."

No one says a word.

◈

An hour later, Holly and I are sitting at the kitchen table drinking tea—orange spice for me, burdock for her. She is wearing her big white robe, and her arms emerge from the sleeves like shy, ravaged animals. The eczema has surfaced on her neck and throat now, which is why I doubled her dose of PABA and made the burdock tea extra strong. No one likes the taste of burdock, and I am touched that Holly drinks the bitter brew without complaining. More vitamin E? I am thinking. Brewer's yeast?

It's not like her to sit here idle—she should be reading, or using her carving tools, or drawing up plans for the hall. My stomach tightens as I look at the streaks on her neck, and her arms so thin and red. She is no better, after all these weeks at home. The medicines aren't working, and the dog hasn't helped at all.

As if summoned by my thoughts, Fawn appears in the doorway. There is no escaping those dark, bottomless eyes.

"What does she want?" I mutter, more to myself than to Holly. And I am stunned when Holly answers right away, in a voice flat with truth: "She wants to know what to do with herself. She wants to know how to be a dog."

◈

I am not surprised that night to reach out and find Holly gone from our bed. I lie there a moment, picturing her on the porch, her arms encircling her knees, her face turned toward the moon shining behind blue clouds, and then I put on my robe and head down the hall. At the entrance to the kitchen, I stop. The back door is open, and in its frame I see Holly and Fawn sitting on the steps. Holly's arms are clasped around the dog. "You have to run." She is sobbing, her face pressed into Fawn's neck. "Please, please run."

I have seen Holly cry, of course, but not like this.

A slow wedge of fear moves into my chest as I turn and edge back down the hall. There is nothing left to draw on. We are bankrupt, stranded.

◈

I leave the house early the next morning, before Holly gets up. I am anxious to get to work, to be in a place where the problems can be solved. Today I need to clean out the compressors and check the bulk food bins—a customer said the oats were stale.

I drive down our dirt road, swerving past the potholes, and turn left into town. Not many kids stop by anymore—we live too far out, but when we had the house on Fulton Street they were always around. They'd come to view Holly's miniatures, or to learn how to make salt crystals, or to see the rescued wildlife convalescing in our backyard. Children can't get enough of Holly. They drop their guard, say things; they forget she's a grownup.

Again I imagine her on Fifth Avenue, working behind the plate-glass windows, and I think of the dainty gardens and the mini deserts she fashions now, and I see the way she's pared down her life. From Bergdorf Goodman to the Talking Turtle Day Care Center. From the dictates of businessmen to the needs of children. There must be clues in this, tips I can use to help her, and as I ponder them, I drive right past my store.

I have finished with the compressors and am on my way to the bulk bins when I notice several people standing out front. The store doesn't open for another twenty minutes, but they can't wait. Just being near these herbs and vitamins, just smelling that wheatgrass makes them feel better, fills them with faith and resolve. I unlock the door of my magic kingdom and let them all inside.

People who shop here generally fall into one of two categories: those who exude good health and those who endlessly pursue it. Today there is one bodybuilder who buys a pound of creatine powder and is in and out of the store so fast I feel used; a fortysomething woman who buys a half-dozen veggie burgers and looks great in spandex; a teenage boy asking about herbal aphrodisiacs; a pale girl with acne who will wander the aisles for over an hour; and, of course Rick, the store mascot, a strapping old man who comes in daily for a pint of carrot juice and who I swear has the life span of a redwood.

Today everybody leaves the store happily clutching their antidotes. I have listened and instructed, have drawn straight lines between the complaints and the cures, like those exercises in grammar school where you match up corresponding subjects. Not all days are this gratifying, especially lately, and instead of feeling fraudulent, guilty over the prices I'm forced to charge, I am pleased with myself as I lock up Earthly Goods. It *is* a place of magic, of hope, and people like Rick and the spandex woman are walking testimonials to the legitimacy of my trade.

I take my time driving home, reluctant to face Holly and the dog and the mire we're in. Again I picture Holly sobbing on the porch, and I'm appalled by the things I don't know about her. Just how close is she to depletion?

And so I'm amazed to open the front door and find her

humming in the hallway. She has a tape measure in her hands and is writing down figures on a piece of paper.

I smile at her. "The diorama?"

She walks up and kisses me. "I'm trying to decide if I should do just one period or a progression of three—Triassic, Jurassic, and Cretaceous."

"The progression," I answer.

"I knew you'd say that," she says.

◈

I am slicing up spinach leaves for an omelet, and Holly is sitting at the table looking through her natural history books.

"Hadrosaurs had rookeries like birds," she informs me. "Their nests were ten feet in diameter."

I smack the flat of my knife against a garlic clove and pull off the papery skin. I am learning a lot about dinosaurs. But there is something else I want to talk about right now. I brush the garlic slivers into the hot skillet, and the fragrance fills the kitchen.

"You know," I begin carefully, casually, "maybe it's not important, getting Fawn to run. If she doesn't want to, maybe we shouldn't try. I mean, hasn't she had enough of that?"

"It's not the same thing," Holly says without turning around.

"If we walk her every day," I persist, "and watch her diet, she won't get fat."

Holly has no comment to this, but I see the resolution in her shoulders, and I know I can't change her mind and probably shouldn't try—she's the expert when it comes to injury.

◈

We are clearing the dinner dishes from the table when Fawn enters the kitchen. She doesn't pause on the threshold this time; she walks right in and sits, and then she does something that startles all three of us. She lifts her chin and makes a sound, a single ardent note, something between a howl and a bark, a question and a statement. Afterward, puzzled, she looks behind her, as if she's not sure where the sound came from. A fork slides off the plate in my hands and clatters on the floor. Holly turns to me, her face radiant.

"She's coming around."

◆

Fawn's recovery happens by degrees, one tenuous achievement every day or so. Yesterday her tail wagged, not exuberantly and not for long—just a few soft beats against the carpet while Holly was petting her—but a breakthrough nevertheless. And just this morning she walked over to the table where I was doing paperwork and rested her slender muzzle on my thigh. I stared at it the way you would a butterfly that lights, oblivious, on the back of your hand.

Fawn even looks better. Although she hasn't gained weight, she seems more solid, more sure of her place in this house. There is a loosening in her now, as if the tension that bound her, that made her a race dog, is finally letting go.

Ten times a night she ran. Ten times around a floodlit track. Sometimes, when she is sleeping on her bed in the living room, I see her legs twitch and I wonder if she is still haunted by those nights—or if the dreams are pleasant, if she is running not around a track, muzzled and numbered, but across a vast meadow, achieving in her sleep a freedom otherwise out of reach. People who are paralyzed have dreams like this. Sleep can be a place for solutions.

And Holly is better, too. Maybe it's because of the dog; maybe they struck some bargain that rock-bottom night on the porch. Then again, I can't rule out the PABA, or all that burdock tea. In any event, the rash is leaving. The marvel occurs at night, in time-lapse; each morning is cause to celebrate. It's a drama we've seen many times before, and still we feel triumphant. How long this state of grace will last is a question we don't need answered.

◈

Like most long-awaited phenomena, it happens without warning. We are walking along the perimeter of the soccer field, as we do every week, Holly near the fence, me on the inside, and Fawn in perfect step between us. Holly is explaining why dinosaurs could not have been cold-blooded when Fawn stops short. We look down at her, surprised, not yet knowing what it could mean.

She springs forward, checks herself, and with a last glance at Holly she is bounding away, jackknifing over the field. Holly reaches for my arm, and all we can do is watch as Fawn leaves us farther and farther behind. In seconds she has reached the edge of the woods and is turning back, closing in fast, racing without a reason, her body in a full ecstatic stretch high above the ground.

Beyond the Strandline

Mary Akers

Everything made Walt angry: the too-hot sun beating down on his bare head, the stranded dolphins in the nearby shallows, the dead one they'd been too late to save, the overeager volunteers, and now this zealous young interviewer. Fifteen months after Chelsea's accident, the sight of a healthy woman still made him angry.

He held out his hands, thick palms facing up. "I'm no candy-ass bunny hugger," he said. "I mean, look at me."

And she *did* look. Stared with her eager, shiny face all turned up to his as if he were some font of freaking knowledge, as if he—Walt Glenny—had all the answers.

He cocked his head, gave her a sideways glance. "Where'd you say you were from again?"

"Did I? Atlanta, originally. But I—"

"No, no. Just now, I mean. Who sent you—the interview?"

"Oh." She giggled and ducked her head. "Sorry. Dolphin Shoals. The institute there. You know them?"

Oh, Walt knew them, all right. They touted marine mammal rescue as a way to up their enrollment but were useless during any real missions. Walt had butted heads with them on more than one occasion, touchy-feely bunch of do-gooders.

"I do," he said. "Better leave it at that." It wasn't as if he wanted to make nice with a Dolphin Shoals rep, but he'd spouted off lately to enough media worms who'd twisted his words and made him out as some sort of vigilante. He'd try keeping his mouth shut for a change. Chelsea would approve—if he could ever tell her and get some sort of meaningful response again, which he couldn't.

"I'm so excited to finally meet you," the interviewer said. "I mean, I've heard so much about you and all."

So that was it. She'd come for an interview, yes, but also meant to worship at the fins of the great dolphin rescuer, maybe even offer herself up to him before the day was out.

And Walt? He couldn't care less. Oh, her flesh filled up her skin nicely enough; smooth and rounded, she was, with shiny straight hair that smelled like cooked apples. Not a knockout, no, but since when had beauty ever been one of his criteria?

"Heard a lot, have you?"

"It's totally inspiring. Helping dolphins like you do—fighting for them, and all, while your wife … " Her voice trailed off.

Yes, there was that. He understood Chelsea's accident made him a tragic figure, but he'd never wanted that, never asked for it, and in the end all the sympathy did was make him angry. Just like this little girl made him angry in some way too complex to name.

There was a time—not so long ago—when he'd have

had her out behind the dive shed, all quivery and tender in his hands, getting life and youth from her like some damned infusion, but not anymore. He just plain didn't have it in him.

"It's a sad fact," he said, crossing his leathery, tanned forearms, white hairs bristling between his fingers. "But they do need help. You'd be surprised what-all humans'll do just to put on a show."

She took a step closer. "I think it's amazing that you're so committed."

Walt switched to his lecture voice. "In Japan they stage huge roundups, bang hammers against steel poles in the water and herd hundreds of dolphins into pens. It's a god-awful noise." He gave her a meaningful look and said, "Dolphins are echolocators."

She nodded with a pretty, blank expression.

"Sonar?" he tried.

She sighed.

"Think of the pain." He touched his ear. "Herders pick the healthiest ones and sell 'em to dolphinariums as performers, or to swim-with programs, even if it means taking a nursing baby from its mother. The rest get bludgeoned and harpooned. The dolphins panic and thrash around—the whole bay turns red."

"Can't you stop them?"

"I've tried. And I'll keep trying, but the herders get violent if they see you videotaping—dolphin roundups make too much money. The killed dolphins get cut up into steaks. In Japan, I'm talking about. And what the poor slobs over there don't realize is dolphin meat's about the most contaminated thing a person could eat—heavy-duty mercury poisoning." Walt raised an eyebrow. "You writing this down?"

She gave him a coy smile. "I've got a photographic memory."

"But I'm *talking*."

"I'll remember. I heard that dolphins are the only species besides humans that actually have, you know—sex. For fun. Is that true?"

The girl—*what was her name again?*—slipped a foot out of its sandal and swirled her bright red toenails in the sand.

Damn, Walt was tired. And this young blonde ball of sex and energy made him even more tired. "How about you tell me what that has to do with these dolphins?" He pointed to the gray shapes in the nearby shallows, draped with wet sheets, surrounded by volunteers dipping and pouring seawater, speaking in soothing tones. "You think they're thinking about sex?"

Her eyes flicked up at him, and she jerked her foot back—hurt, he guessed. Not that he had time to worry about little girls' feelings. Better off, these days, if they learned early.

"No." She spoke in a closed-off, spoiled-child's voice.

Amber—*was that the name she'd given him?*—well, she was mad now, little Amber was, but better mad than courting sex from a man old enough to be her father.

And Walt wasn't *old*. He could still do more push-ups at fifty-five than most men half his age. He could wrestle a panicked dolphin into calm, organize a group of hysterical do-gooders with a barked order, and sweet-talk the big money folks into donating. Everyone knew who manned the helm at the Alliance for Dolphin Freedom. The ADF *was* Walt Glenny. And he meant to teach the world that dolphin capture and use was akin to slavery, every bit as bad as the human kind.

"Didn't you used to capture them?"

He sighed. "Yes, and I've seen firsthand the damage. That's why I work so hard to stop it. Now if you'll excuse me, I'll be getting back." He about-faced and strode away.

As he reached his truck, the pink-skinned Canadian woman—discoverer of the stranded dolphins—ran up to him. She was plenty older than the interviewer but just as eager, captivated by her own ideas of what she wanted dolphins to be. Fading blonde hair hung in wet strings about her face. Her smile, big and horsey, dominated the rest of her sharp features, and her bathing suit sagged at her breasts.

"You're leaving?" she asked, holding his door as he tried to shut it.

Walt remembered her name well enough: Sonya. Like sonogram. Fish finder, baby finder, blood clot finder—the damned thing they used when they opened up Chelsea's skull to look inside, after she collapsed thirty feet below the surface and he got her—somehow—to the beach, picking her up when the water no longer supported her, dropping his own tank and resting her head on the warm sand just beyond the strandline. Then Chelsea lying slack in the emergency room, still in her bikini, sand all stuck to one side of her face—right on her *eyeball*, for Christ's sake—and half in her mouth as they wheeled her away. Chelsea's pretty face, already collapsing in on itself, told him more right then than anything the doctors would say later.

And as hard as that memory was, it was still better than the ones his brain was making now: Chelsea's wasted body after fifteen sunless months tucked under starched white hospital sheets beneath buzzing fluorescent lights, all traces of sand long since washed away, her hair thin and clumpy, white scalp showing through the coarse gray roots that had grown halfway down into the brown.

She would've hated that.

He retrieved his sunglasses from the dash. "Listen, I gotta run get the van. Can't carry a dolphin off in this." He pointed to the truck bed behind him. "Van's got a sling—doesn't bruise the dolphin."

"Bruise?" Sonya cocked her head like a sandpiper and studied the motionless dolphin. "Isn't she dead?"

"Yeah, dead." He gave Sonya a withering look, then

thought better of it and rearranged his face. "You want any bruising to be from trauma *before* death. Autopsy tells a story that way."

During the recent months of Chelsea's *illness* (as that infernally Bible-thumping sister of hers continued to call it), Walt found himself wishing that day of diving *had* been fatal. At the moment of crisis, when Chelsea looked at him through her mask, eyes big and panic stricken, he thought he was doing the right thing rushing her to Marathon, to the emergency room—but fifteen months of limbo-hell later it seems as if he should have just let her finish out her last breaths there on the sand with the warm sun beating down on her.

Chelsea always hated air-conditioning. It took years of living under her rules, but he finally got used to nothing more than a ceiling fan. Now, visiting Chelsea in the meat-locker hospital for as little as ten minutes left him fighting off a subterranean chill for hours.

"It was just so strange," said Sonya, "seeing those dolphins close to the shore, all in one place, clicking and clicking like that. They must have been saying 'Get up, get up,' or something. Anyway, when I got closer I saw the dead one at the bottom. So sad."

Walt knew dolphins. Hell, he could practically speak their language after thirty-plus years of working with them. First watching them ride the bow waves as a merchant marine en route to Vietnam, then helping capture dolphins and train them to perform at Ocean World, followed by a stint with the Navy training dolphins to place underwater charges, always looking for some way of working with them that didn't feel so wrong.

Then finally, after one of his girls—Britta, a spotted dolphin he'd helped capture and train—died in his arms, it was as if the blinders came off, and he could see how badly the animals missed the wild, how depressed they became when they were captured and forced to eat dead fish handed to them, how often the dolphins died. People assumed performing dolphins were happy, smiling things, but the sad truth was that performing dolphins didn't live long, and turnover was high. Dolphinariums always trotted out the odd twenty-year-veteran performer who smiled and chirped for the spectators and made everyone believe it was a good life, free of dangers and disease, but that wasn't the norm. And hell, some slaves didn't want their freedom, either, even after the Civil War—begged their masters to keep them on. Some kidnapping victims came to side with their violent captors. It didn't make it *right.*

"Can I help?" asked Sonya. "I mean, I can come with you."

He shook his head, then thought, *What the hell?* "I guess there's no harm in a tagalong," he said. Then he added, "Other side's open," in a gentler voice. Sonya scrambled around the truck and climbed in.

◈

Shortly after Chelsea's accident, when the words *persistent vegetative state* were spoken, the women began to throw themselves at Walt. There was nothing to explain it. No change other than Chelsea's affliction. He was the same man all the time—a squat man, really, taking after his shovel-handed father, who worked his life away in the coal mines of Norton, Virginia—his father with the broad, flat, Neanderthal forehead and shoulders like a damned plank.

The first woman to approach him was a neighbor, a young redheaded widow who brought him a soufflé, arriving at the door in a see-through black shirt with no bra. He'd been too shocked to appreciate the gesture at the time. Too shocked, also, when she sidled up to him and rubbed her left breast against his arm. All he could think was, *Soufflé? What kind of man eats soufflé the day his wife gets diagnosed a vegetable?* And she took her cherry-red nipples home with her that night, untouched, but by the end of the week she was back, and this time he didn't let the gesture go to waste. He knew it was pity sex, but there was something cathartic about it just the same, something cleansing about accepting this woman's offering: her body a sacrificial object for his healing. Something primitive made him feel that, yes, he was a man still, alive still, sexual still, *not* dying, not wasting away in that hospital bed on those white, white sheets beside his brain-dead wife.

It came easier after the first. *My wife's a vegetable* the mutually acknowledged shorthand giving women permission to soothe his pain. Walt wasn't exactly proud of the long string of soothers whose offers he'd accepted, but he wasn't ashamed, either. Pain was pain, and the only way to make it stop was to give the body what it wanted. And besides, he made the women feel good. It wasn't as if they left unhappy.

And so it went. Until the doctor finally tap-danced around the idea of removing all life support, feeding tube included. Walt agreed. Neither he nor Chelsea had wanted to live life as a vegetable; they'd talked about it even, just never written anything down. But once the decision was officially made, he'd felt purposeful and good; he was finally honoring Chelsea's wishes.

And that was the turning point. He stopped bedding every woman with a soft eye for his predicament. He stopped using his persistently vegetative wife as a tool of seduction. Just stopped. Cold. And he couldn't say precisely why, but it relieved some sense of burden he'd been experiencing, took away the elephant he hadn't even known was sitting on his chest.

Meanwhile, Chelsea's stupid, thick-headed sister continued to believe it was only a matter of time before Chelsea recovered, and she fought Walt's decision at every turn. In her eyes, he was a cold-blooded killer, when all he wanted was to finally give his wife's worn-out body a little peace.

No one could say he hadn't done right by Chelsea. No one. He had been there from the beginning. He visited her every day, even sold off the furniture and moved to a dingy apartment in Marathon to be closer to the hospital. He exercised her arms and legs the way the physical therapist taught him, talked to her blank face about life outside the hospital the way the nurses said might help. But that body in the bed wasn't Walt's wife any more than that dolphin carcass on the beach was. He knew Chelsea's smile. And that once-in-a-blue-moon spasm that twisted up what was left of her face wasn't it. She couldn't even eat, for crying out loud. Couldn't swallow her own spit. Wore a diaper. And that crimped tube they squirted liquid food into, that nasty tunnel that led right to her stomach? That was the most barbaric thing of all. He would've rather seen her eaten by a shark.

◆

"It's all hinked up," Walt said as Sonya tugged and twisted at the seat belt. "Might as well just click it in. You won't get it righted."

"Well, you be sure and drive carefully then," she said, with what passed for a coquettish—if horsey—smile. "Yes?"

He looked at her sideways. She wasn't half bad from that angle.

"Yes," he said.

Then he thought about the fact that he'd have to find the time to swing by the hospital to manipulate Chelsea's limbs. Or no, no he wouldn't. The feeding tube was out now. Couldn't he finally admit that moving her arms and legs wouldn't matter? But her remaining days were numbered; he needed to stop by for that simple reason, manipulation or not. He turned to Sonya. "You care if I run by the hospital first?"

"The hospital? Can they help?"

"Not for the dolphins. My wife's there."

"Your wife?"

"Had a stroke a year and a half ago."

Sonya brought her hand to her mouth, covering her teeth. "I had no idea. I'm so sorry." She turned toward Walt. "Is it horrible?"

He gave her an appraising look. "You're the first one to ask *that*. I thought I'd heard them all."

"I just mean … it must be. Yes?"

He tightened his grip on the wheel and turned into the hospital parking lot. A row of palm trees clattered their fronds in a hot breeze off the blacktop. He pulled into a Visitors space and shut the engine.

"Yes," he said.

"Mind if I come with? I've got a cover-up in my bag. It's too hot out here."

He nodded. "Suit yourself."

Outside Chelsea's door, Sonya touched his arm. "I'll wait here." She cranked her head toward a row of yellow Naugahyde sofas.

Walt stepped into the room, moved over to the bed, and took Chelsea's hand, rubbing the fingers. "Hey, Chels," he said. "Sweetheart."

He had long ago stopped asking questions. No "How are you?" No "What's up?" The silence that followed a question was too all encompassing. It sucked the air out of a room.

"You look good." His standard line. Really, she looked like hell. Three days without the feeding tube or even water had left her skin a pasty gray. Her lips were flaking, and he reached for the jar of Vaseline and spread a greasy layer over them. "I can only come a few more times, honey, then I'll be … "

Unfinished sentences didn't matter either. It was all the same now. During their marriage, whenever Walt told a story that rambled on for too long, Chelsea would lean toward him and roll her hands in a move-it-along signal that told him he was losing focus. He hated it at the time. Now he longed for it.

"Here, let me." He lifted her limp hands, held them at the wrists, and attempted to do the hand roll. "Move it along, Walt," he said, in a high falsetto.

Not that Chelsea's voice was ever high. It was sexy-deep. Or maybe he just remembered it that way. Hard to say. Memories had a way of going fuzzy and indistinct much faster than you ever thought they could. Now he was the husband of a voiceless wife. He guessed that the underlying plumbing still worked so that technically she *could* talk. If she had the air and the will and the muscle control and the brain to back the voice box up. The real irony was, Walt had never been the sort of husband who wanted his wife to *just shut up*. They'd talked all the time—about meaningless shit some days, but also about real, gut-wrenching stuff.

How the hell he ended up in this ridiculous melodrama of a life was beyond him. Bent on saving dolphins when he couldn't even save his own wife. No wonder women saw him as a tragic figure. Hell, that's exactly what he was. He'd be happy to quit the ADF if he could. But the dolphins were his job—his mission. He was the head and founder of the whole organization. He couldn't quit his reason for being. He just had to wait it out was all. Wait for life after Chelsea. See what that held.

Walt pinched the space between his eyes. He leaned over, gave Chelsea a kiss. A trail of Vaseline—he hated the stuff—slimed his lips, but he lingered an extra moment, then wiped the back of his hand across his mouth and turned to leave.

When he pulled the privacy curtain aside, Chelsea's sister

Bea was standing there. Her face, with its echo of Chelsea's, disconcerted him every time.

"Murderer," she said, by way of greeting. "Come to finish the job yourself?"

"Fuck off." Walt wiped his nose. Vaseline smeared across his cheek.

"I want you to know, I've filed a motion to stop you from killing her."

The words took a moment to sink in. "You what?"

"Tomorrow, expect a court order to replace the feeding tube. I won't let you do this. You don't own her."

Walt wished for a moment that he *were* a murderer. Bea would be his first victim. His fingertips twitched with the terrible urge to encircle her throat and squeeze. "Chelsea never wanted this. It isn't natural."

"Don't you tell me what's natural—you want to starve an innocent woman to death. Your *wife*. That's natural?"

Bea's voice was shrill. Walt wondered if he could have her physically removed from the hospital. Would security do that for him? Would they be on his side? Would he be the ultimate bastard if he did that? Did it even matter anymore? His ties with Chelsea's family had long since been broken. "How 'bout we don't do this in front of Chels," he said, trying like hell to take the high road.

"Wouldn't you like that? Don't think she doesn't know you're trying to kill her. She does. I've told her, and she knows. Just look at her face." Bea swung her arm in an arc that ended at Chelsea's bedside. "Look."

Walt looked, and what he saw was the same thing he'd seen the first time he visited her, and the same thing he'd seen every day since: a shell. Not a spark of his wife. Nothing.

◈

"Who was that woman?" Sonya asked when they were back in the truck.

"Sister-in-law."

"She didn't look too happy."

Walt pulled the truck up close to the warehouse and cut the motor. The air in the cab began to get hot immediately. He turned to Sonya. "Her freako-religious cult of a church does chanting and laying-on-of-hands in the hospital and expects a miracle any day. It would have driven Chelsea mad. She'd kick 'em out before they even got their Bibles open. Instead she just lies there while they pray and sprinkle holy water on her. It's all for themselves. A fat lot of good it does her. She can't even tell them to fuck off."

Walt opened the truck door and stepped out. Sonya didn't move.

He leaned back in. "You coming?"

"Should we be getting back?"

"Key to the van's in the warehouse. I've got in-water volunteers for the next three hours. The only thing left is to cart the carcass to the lab; I'll wait on daylight for that."

Inside, Walt flipped the light switch; the bulbs hummed then flickered to life. Sonya blinked in the sudden brightness.

"You don't believe in God?"

Walt sighed. "Not Bea's God." He moved deeper into the warehouse, guiding Sonya by the elbow. She reached across and placed her hand over his; her fingers were cool.

Damn Bea for getting the lawyers involved. Walt didn't have the money to fight her in court, and, frankly, the possibility that he would have to do such a thing in order to let Chelsea die a natural death hadn't even occurred to him. What was worse, Walt sure as hell didn't have the money to pay for another year of hospital care at $300-plus a day. Which begged an even bigger question: How the hell had *life* come down to *money*?

"You okay?" Sonya leaned forward to look into his eyes.

"Fine," he said, though his throat felt as if it were locked in a vise.

"No, you aren't." Sonya's eyes were big and blue, and they welled up with the tears that Walt should have been shedding. "It's okay," she said.

"You're the one who's crying."

"I don't know why."

He reached out and took her hand. "Look, I didn't mean—"

At the touch of Walt's hand, Sonya crumpled. Her shoulders dropped forward and shrugged with sudden sobs. "It's just—" She choked on the words and swallowed hard. "It's just, I can't picture my own husband—back home—he wouldn't—if it were me, and it just—it isn't. I'm sorry. I'm so stupid." She wiped furiously at her eyes.

"It's all right," said Walt, stepping forward, secure again in what was required of him. He knew this one, at least: The woman cries, and the man holds her. He could do this much.

Sonya moved gratefully into the embrace. "I'm sorry," she mumbled, scrubbing her face into his shoulder. "You don't need this." He felt the wetness seeping through his T-shirt.

"Shh." Walt cupped her more tightly. He hadn't held a crying woman since Chelsea, and it felt good, suddenly, to be on the other side—moving from the *comforted* to the *comforter*. It felt right. He put his palm against the back of Sonya's head and brought her in close. Her hair felt thin and soft beneath his fingers.

Sonya leaned back. When she opened her eyes, Walt saw that they were red-rimmed and puffy. Streaks of color spread down her cheeks. Ragged breaths made her chest rise and fall unevenly. She smiled, but her eyes kept searching his with the look of a cornered animal.

Some desperateness in Sonya's face, some rawness of

emotion washing over her, just inches from his own face, broke through Walt's calm, and he leaned forward to give her a kiss, just a light press of comfort. But when their lips touched, she grabbed his head and pulled forward greedily, opening his mouth with her own parted lips. Walt felt the blood pounding in his temples.

With a handful of hair in his fist he moved her head toward his, mashing their mouths together. Their teeth scraped awkwardly. It was more about unbridled energy than passion, but she moaned and pressed into him, pushing him against a row of high drawers. The knobs dug into his back. She tore at his clothing with a grunt of frustration.

Despite his discomfort, Walt felt himself growing hard. It felt good—in the way of a cold beer on a hot day—a liquid filling-up. He slid a hand beneath her bikini top.

Walt didn't want this woman, he hadn't lusted after her, but at the same time he did want her. He craved the wild, bucking nature of her, the roller coaster, the crazy abandon, the release. It was like a drug surging through his veins, this insane, angry desire.

Sonya mumbled into Walt's open mouth. Her breath was hot in his; she tasted of peaches.

"Mmm?" He didn't really care what she said. Didn't care what might be spoken. What could she say at this point but yes? There was no going back. He kissed her deeply, filling her mouth with his tongue.

Sonya pulled away, gasping. She took a deep breath, and Walt watched her face soften.

"I saw you with her," she said. "I looked in while you were there." Her eyes were heavy-lidded, her cheeks flushed. "It was amazing. So beautiful. So—"

She took another deep breath and brought her mouth back passionately to Walt's, but he kept still. For the briefest moment, it was a parody—the ready female pressing herself against the male, the male standing like a stone, refusing her.

◈

"You can come up," Sonya repeated, not opening the van door. "I would let you stay. You know that. Yes?"

Walt reached across in front of her and pulled the handle. The door swung open with a creak.

"Yes," he said.

When the hotel door closed on Sonya's retreating back, it was fully dark; a halo of night insects swarmed an outdoor globe. Walt pulled away from the parking lot and returned to the stranded dolphins. His job. He knew he shouldn't have been gone so long, but Nick, his main volunteer, was a smart kid, trustworthy.

Traffic on Route 1 was minimal; Walt made a U-turn and parked on the side of the roadway. Nick met him halfway to the beach.

"Mimi and Ralph are gone."

"What?" Walt shook his head. "Dead?" The two older dolphins—a mated pair, he suspected—had been gaining strength over the course of the day. How had they deteriorated so quickly?

"No." Nick laughed. "I mean gone. They swam off."

"Off?" Dolphins rarely left a sick or stranded pod member. They usually stayed to the bitter end, even becoming casualties themselves. "They just left?"

"Well, yeah. Amber and Stacy were in the water, and the dolphins started making noises, and then they just squirmed out of their hands. They eased off like they'd planned it, then surfaced farther out. They're getting around okay, too."

"Good. One for the record books. How about Lulu?" Lulu was the youngest and sickest of the dolphins; she had suffered a case of severe sunburn prior to being covered by Walt and his volunteers. Most likely the sunburn—a deadly condition for dolphins—had further weakened her.

"Lulu's not doing so hot. She's breathing, but it's slowed way down. She's pretty unresponsive."

"Damn. All right. Thanks, Nick." Walt clapped the younger man on the shoulder. "You look beat, man. Go home—all three of you. I got it from here. You guys get some shut-eye. I might need you tomorrow."

"Who'll take Lulu's watch?"

"I'll stay with her."

"All night?"

"Yeah, I got it."

"And that one?" Nick angled his head toward the carcass on the sand.

"We'll have enough volunteers in the morning. I can deliver it anytime after first light."

Walt returned to the van, donned his wetsuit and booties, then trudged through the waist-high water.

"I've got it from here," he said, placing his palms under the dolphin and nodding to Amber.

"Thanks." She dropped her shoulders and rolled her head. "I'm stiff. And cold."

"Get some rest," said Walt.

"You don't need me?"

"Nope. Come back at first light. I can use you then."

"Can we finish the interview tomorrow?"

For a moment Walt was confused. Had that really only been today? "Sure, sure," he said. "We'll finish, no problem."

Amber waded to shore. With a protective hand at the small of her back, Nick guided her up the beach. They walked to the road together. *Good,* thought Walt, she'd found a far better receptacle for her considerable affections.

After Nick's beat-up Volkswagen roared to life and moved

off down the road, Walt was alone with the ocean. Exactly where he liked to be. Soft waves pulled at his legs then moved on, small ribbons of phosphorescence sliding onto the sand. If there were sounds other than the water lapping against Walt and Lulu, of water rolling over itself to shore, he couldn't hear them. Being alone in the ocean felt like moving back through time to meet the origins of life. Walt could be a one-celled phytoplankton, or a floating jelly, or an intertidal fish using its fins like feet for the first time.

And Walt was with Lulu. He could feel the faint pulse of her heart against his palm. Her blowhole opened and closed laboriously in intervals that were much too long. Each exhalation was a blast of moist air; he could feel the effort as her lungs pushed old air out and pulled new in. The dolphin was giving up. The accrued weight of her body had increased, like a baby slipping into sleep, its mass heavier for the slackness. Walt's shoulders already tingled from the strain.

Was she suffering?

He had no doubt that animals suffered; that wasn't the question. No. He wondered if Lulu was suffering, here and now. Only one side of a dolphin's brain sleeps at a time—one side rests; the other side keeps watch, stays alert. So, was there a portion of the brain devoted specifically to suffering? Could the suffering section sleep all the time? Was there a neurological setting for near-death that allowed a body to feel no pain?

If Chelsea's brain had worked independently, functioning side-by-side with itself, would she, after the stroke, still have had one good side left? Would she even now have a waking side for Walt?

Walt had held a dying dolphin in his arms before. He knew the signs. What to do about the dying was the question he faced. What to do. Did he owe Lulu some sort of *death duty* as a compassionate fellow creature? If so, what was it? Stay with her and keep her company as she died? Pet her? Talk to her? Offer solace? Was he obligated to try, stubbornly, to keep her alive, despite her obvious instinctual attempts to die? Or was the better course to leave the dolphin completely alone and let nature take its own in a way that Walt—outsider—could never comprehend?

In the end, he talked to the dolphin. He stroked the smooth area under Lulu's pectoral fins, beneath which her fragile heart stammered on.

"You're a pretty girl, aren't you?" Walt murmured. "I bet you love to swim and catch fish and play with your family. You're a smart girl, too. Yes, Lulu's a smart girl. A smart girl and a pretty girl." He pulled one hand away, keeping her blowhole above the waterline by a light touch on her underbelly.

"But I think it's time. And I should let you go, shouldn't I, Lulu?" He pulled his remaining hand away slowly. "Hmm? Do you want me to?" The water slid up the gray sides of her flanks and edged toward the blowhole. "Do you, Lulu?" Walt put his head close to hers and asked, "Yes?"

Meat

C.S. Malerich

I was six when we got Meat. That's what we named her because Mom said, "That's what she's going to be." She didn't want us to get attached, and she told Dad not to get sentimental and suggest something like "Patches" instead.

The neighbors thought it was a great joke. I remember Mrs. Beauchamp leaning over the back fence to get her first good look at Meat and chuckling when I told her Meat's name. Dad was kind of the neighborhood oddball and old hippie because we were the only family on the block to have an electric car and our own composting toilet. But the local newspaper ran a story for suburbanites about raising your own farm animals, so we couldn't be the only ones in the world.

It started because all four of us—Mom, Dad, my sister, and me—were leaving the grocery store and we ran into a group of animal rights people holding a demonstration on the sidewalk. Four of them had big posters with pictures of animals that were crowded together, dirty with mud and feces, and pressing against the bars that held them in. Two demonstrators were handing out bright flyers, and one had a bullhorn telling everyone, "This is how the animals live and die. This is the cost of your meat."

I didn't know what was going on, but I knew there was something exciting happening. I liked animals, and there were animals on those posters. That's all I saw and understood. I would have gone right up to the people who were making the commotion, except Mom grabbed my hand and my sister's, and she told us, "Don't talk to them." Dad's hands were full, though, holding reusable bags of groceries, and Mom only had two hands, so she couldn't stop *him* from going over and talking to the demonstrators.

That night, Dad wouldn't eat his ribs at dinner, and Mom was furious.

"Isn't it enough we spend twice as much on organic?" she asked, dropping her fork.

Dad didn't want to argue in front of my sister and me, but later I heard him say to Mom while they were doing the dishes, "It is wrong, don't you think, to treat animals like that? After all, they've got feelings, too."

"What do you mean? You think if I was sick, or one of the girls, you wouldn't kill an animal to save them? You'd put some dumb beast ahead of your own family?"

"No, no," said Dad. "That's not what I'm saying."

So Dad was quieter than normal and only picked at his dinner the rest of the week, until he came home Friday with the idea for Meat. He had the story from the newspaper, and clippings from magazines, and a pamphlet about urban farmers and sustainable agriculture, and articles he'd printed off the Internet from a website called The Ethical Eater.

Mom read everything he put in front of her, and in the end she still thought the home-raised, humane movement was stupid. This wasn't as simple as building a compost pile or buying fair-trade chocolate. It was going to make a lot of work for her, and she asked: "The kids are going to get attached, and then what?"

But she could tell this was Dad's way of compromising, and she went along with it for his sake.

◈

Meat was about my size when we got her, and clever, too. She learned her way around the house in one afternoon, and how to open and close the doors the next day. So we couldn't keep her in and had to give her the run of the yard. Mom didn't think Meat was going to last in the middle of the suburbs, but she learned pretty quick not to step off the curb into the street, or to cross into Mr. Catrone's flower beds next door. The rest of the neighbors had fences, so Meat was safe from them and from speeding cars. And the neighbors got used to Meat.

"A little experiment," Dad told Mrs. Beauchamp over the back fence. "Raising our own food." He explained how bad factory farms were and how he wanted us to understand the circle of life and respect animals.

"Like the Indians," said Mrs. Beauchamp, catching on, "using every bit of the animal and thanking its spirit and all that?"

"Exactly!" said Dad. He didn't even bother correcting her to say, "Native Americans."

"Hmm," murmured Mrs. Beauchamp. "Wonder if the meat tastes any different?"

"That's what I've read," said Dad. "An animal that's lived a calm, happy life releases fewer stress hormones. The flesh tastes better, and it's better for you."

◈

My sister was eleven now, getting secretive and standoffish, and she was embarrassed if I talked to her at school in front of her friends. I didn't care, though, because I had Meat. It was spring, and the weather was mild, and I would have been outside all the time anyway, but Meat was also out in the yard now. So we were together from the start. She was my new toy and my new playmate. In no time, I'd taught her basic hide-and-seek and tag. We showed Dad, and he laughed out loud and told us both how smart we were. I heard him tell Mom, standing on the patio, "See, this is good for her. She's learning responsibility. It's like what 4-H used to do." But Mom grew up in the city, far away from 4-H clubs, and she'd learned responsibility when she forgot to lock up her bike and it got stolen. Mom turned around and walked inside.

I'm not sure what I was learning, but I do know, when I came home every day after school, Meat was the first one I looked for, and we were together the rest of the day. I took her everywhere, from the playground at one end of the block to the creek at the other—my whole world. Only at bedtime we separated, me to my room and her to the back porch, where Mom clipped the lead shank to her harness and tied her up for the night.

I don't know who my sister disdained more: me or Meat. The only time I ever heard her speak to Meat was when Meat was sitting on the porch steps, resting after a game of tag. All my sister said was, "Move," so she could get past.

Meat jumped up and took a step down, toward my sister, who pushed Meat out of the way and stomped up the rest of the steps. She slammed the door behind her. It wouldn't have bothered me any, but Meat was bewildered and wouldn't get back to the game after that.

She sulked whenever my sister ignored her. I was her best friend, you see, but Meat liked all of us. Dad liked her back, with the same kind of enthusiastic welcome he showed when the Pakistani couple moved in across the street. He told Meat "good-bye" when he left for work and "hello" when he came home, and he ruffled her hair.

Even Mom warmed up to her after a couple weeks. I saw her pat Meat's head when she didn't think anyone else was looking.

My sister never changed, though. When my teacher at school assigned us to draw a picture of our family, I got a gold star on mine. I showed it to my sister on the school bus.

"This is Mom, and this is Dad. That's me, and that's you, and that's Meat. See, there are five people in our family."

"Don't be an idiot. There are four people in our family."

I used my fingers to check, counting out loud.

That only annoyed her more. "Meat's not part of the family, stupid. As soon as she gets big enough, Mom and Dad are going to send her to the butcher, and she'll be dinner."

"*So?*" I said. Now I was upset. I repeated what Dad had told me: "We feed her and take care of her now, and she'll feed and take care of us later." Perfectly reasonable. "So she *can* be part of the family now!"

My sister snorted. "Some family," she said. "Idiots and phonies." She went to sit with her friends even though the bus was still moving.

◈

At night before bed, I asked Mom and Dad if Meat was part of the family.

"Of course she is," Dad told me. "We love her and take care of her, don't we?"

I had to agree.

"She loves us and wants to take care of us, too, don't you think?"

That, too, was irrefutable.

But Mom didn't say anything, except to ask me if I'd

brushed my teeth. As they left the room, she glared at Dad. "I told you," I heard her say to him in the hallway.

◈

Whatever she said after that, though, it didn't stick. When school let out for the summer, I asked to take charge of feeding Meat. Mom had gotten Meat her own dishes, but I liked it when Meat ate out of my hand, and she did, too.

"No," said Mom. "You'll overfeed her. She's getting too big already."

But Dad said, "Of course you can." He looked at Mom and mouthed, "Responsibility."

We wore Mom down, eventually. So at meals, Meat sat on the floor next to my chair in the dining room, and I fed her off my own plate, instead of Meat eating in the kitchen by herself. My sister insisted on moving her seat, so she could be as far from us as possible. Two nights later, that wasn't even far enough, and she asked to take her dinner to her room. Mom scowled but let her go.

In the fall, Mom told me she'd take over at lunch when I was in school. But I still got up early to give Meat her breakfast, and I still fed her dinner. Dad took this as a sign that the responsibility lessons were sinking in.

◈

While it was warm outside, Mom used the garden hose and the kiddie pool to wash Meat, scrubbing her once a week. But after the first frost, Meat shivered so much and her lips started to turn blue, and Mom said she wouldn't do that again. For a month, Meat went without a bath, and I told Dad she smelled. My sister complained, too. Then, the next time I was in the tub, Meat sat outside the door whining because Dad was out at the school board meeting, and my sister wouldn't pay her any attention, and Mom and I were locked inside the bathroom. So finally, Mom opened the door.

"Well, get in here," she told Meat. "Get in that tub. Might as well clean two with the water for one."

After that, Mom gave us our baths together and used the same bubble bath and shampoo. Meat's hair was thick. Once Mom showed me how, I could spend hours combing and braiding it. Once, on Dad's birthday, I even picked flowers and wove them into a crown for Meat's head. I showed her in the mirror and told her she looked pretty, even though I didn't really think so. She looked vacant and friendly, the way animals do, and she smiled at the mirror without understanding what she was looking at.

"That's you, Dumbo," I said, laughing but not meanly. Dad always said we should think about Meat's feelings and give her a nice life.

◈

Finally I asked if Meat could sleep in my room, and Dad said he didn't see why not. Mom wasn't exactly happy about that either, but she didn't get in the way when Dad set up a bed for Meat next to mine. I guess Mom figured that, since Meat hadn't made any messes on the porch, there wasn't much harm in letting her stay in the house. Plus, the nights were getting colder.

So every night turned into a slumber party for us. I'd tell Meat about school and make fun of my gym teacher and the bald principal and the bullies in my class. I'd tell her all the jokes I'd never make to their faces. Then I'd giggle, and Meat would smile. She was a good listener, and I knew my secrets were safe with her.

◈

She was getting bigger, and she was always expensive to keep. Mom was right. I liked feeding her—and she liked eating—so much that after a year, Meat outweighed me. Dad said it was about time to bring her to the butcher—a special butcher he'd found after research online and phone interviews. He wanted to find someone committed to a respectful, clean death, even if it meant driving fifty miles.

"Which it does," said Mom, sarcastic like she usually was.

At bedtime that night, while Meat was in the bathroom (using the toilet like we'd trained her), Dad asked me if I wanted to go with him to the butcher. Before I could answer, he told me he understood if I wanted to stay at the house instead but that it might be easier for Meat if I came along. "After all, she knows you best—you've taken care of her more than any of us. She'd probably like to have you by her side."

Mom overheard this and didn't like it. "You don't have to go if you don't want to," she told me. "Your feelings matter, too."

But I said I'd go.

Mom looked at me for a long moment. "We'll all go."

Dad frowned. Then he asked me to go for a walk with him the next day after school, so he could talk with me.

◈

Meat enjoyed the car ride. Except for when Dad first brought her home, she hadn't been in a car before. I'd just learned to make pinwheels in arts-and-crafts the day before, and I had two I'd made, one for each of us. We played with these and listened to the *Kidsongs* CD Dad was playing up front. My sister insisted on having the front seat because Mom wouldn't let her stay home by herself, and she was sulking with her earbuds in and her MP3 player blasting loud enough that I could hear forbidden words in the lyrics. Mom must have heard them, too, sitting in the back seat next to me and Meat. But she didn't say anything. I guess one big fight with my sister per day was all she wanted.

Of course, nobody mentioned where we were going. Meat didn't know, and it was so much like family vacations we used to take (before we had to worry about someone taking care of Meat), it was easy for me to forget, too. But when we pulled into a gravel driveway between a store and a barn, I remembered.

The butcher was a big man, but he had a nice face, and he was friendly with Mom and Dad. He thanked them for their business and shook their hands. Dad told me to get out of the car and bring Meat. My sister didn't even unbuckle her seat belt. She stayed put.

As we walked toward the back of the barn, I could hear the butcher explaining in a kind and serious voice, like a doctor's, to Mom and Dad, "I stun her in the temple so she can't feel a thing, then we hang her upside down. One clean cut to the jugular, and she bleeds out in less than a minute. It'll be quick and peaceful."

I'm sure Meat didn't hear, though. Always curious, she was looking around at everything, listening and smelling the air. We were far out in the country now. Beyond the buildings was nothing but hay fields, and the buzzing of insects and birdsong filled up the space. On a different day, we would have had fun exploring and running through those fields. She probably thought that was why we were here, that her family and her best friend were taking her on a nice adventure.

The butcher opened a door at the back of the barn and led us into a small, clean room with a linoleum floor. There was a row of rubber slickers hanging from hooks on the wall, a counter top of tools, and another door. Mom asked me if I wanted to go back to the car and wait, but I said no. I knew when I left, I wouldn't see Meat again. I also knew I couldn't say good-bye because that might upset her. Dad had explained it all to me: Even though Meat wasn't going to live with us anymore, she was going to keep on living *through* us and *for* us. It sounded wonderful, like magic. If Meat could have understood what was going to happen to her—that she was going to become more a part of the family she loved than ever—she'd have been happy. But, Dad said, Meat wouldn't be able to understand, and she'd be scared if she knew she was going to die. So no good-byes. That made sense to me because I'd be scared, too, if I knew I was going to die, and because I didn't really understand the magic part either. I did know it meant I wouldn't see her again, and we wouldn't play together anymore.

So all of us put on rubber slickers except for Meat, and protective goggles over our eyes, and we went into the next room.

◈

Mom told me to hug Meat. I did, and even though Dad had told me not to, I whispered "good-bye" in her ear. When I pulled away, she was confused. And then the butcher came up behind her with his stun gun, and his big hand was on her shoulder. She was still looking at me, and there was no more curiosity and no more confusion. Meat was scared.

The butcher was true to his word, though. It was all over in less than two minutes. He stunned her, lifted her, and hung her by one of the hooks above us. Then he cut her throat. Her eyes were still open—she was still looking at me. Blood came pouring out of her on each side of her head. I wondered if it wasn't too late, if they couldn't stop it and fix her. I half wanted to shout, "Wait!" and find out. Death was a mysterious thing for me. I'd always thought about it like a light switch you flicked off. But here was Meat, not on or off. Dying but not yet dead, living but not able to live anymore.

It was only for a few seconds, and then her eyes got cloudy. And then she was gone. Off. There was some splatter on our slickers and goggles, but most of her blood ran down the sloping floor to a drain.

Dad breathed a sigh. "That was fast," he congratulated the butcher. "And painless. Thank you for your quick work."

I was as numb as if the butcher had stunned me, too. Everything I heard seemed to come from very far away, and every move I made seemed like it was someone else making it.

"You're welcome, of course," said the butcher. "I only do for them what I hope someone will do for me when it's my time." He was escorting us to a third room where we could get cleaned up. It was part of keeping the operation sanitary, he explained, that no one went out the same way they came in.

"Well, you've saved me from a life of vegetarianism," said Dad, half-joking. "Really, I can eat meat again with a clear conscience."

The butcher nodded. "Death is part of life. It's completely natural," he observed. "Some people never come to terms with that. But some life has to end so that other life can begin."

"Exactly," said Dad. "Exactly."

"Now," said the butcher, as he pulled off his goggles, "do you want the hide, hair, and bones as well? That'll be another fifty dollars."

While they talked, I turned back to look for Mom. She hadn't come through the door with us; she was still in the kill room. When I looked, I saw that she'd taken Meat down from the hook. She was holding her against her chest, like the way sometimes she still held me even though I was too big for it. Meat was definitely too big for it.

I didn't want to go back in there. I didn't want to get close to Meat again—or the dead thing that had been Meat. I wasn't sure what Mom was doing. I turned away, and she came out a few minutes later.

◆

When we got back into the car, Mom and I were quiet. My sister looked at us suspiciously, as if waiting for some sign that we'd changed our minds and Meat would, in fact, be coming home with us again, alive as ever.

Dad got into the front seat with another sigh of relief. "Well," he said, "I'm glad I took the time to interview and find the right person. The cuts will be ready next week. I'll come over after work." As he often did as he talked, he seized on an idea and became eager. "We should plan a dinner party, invite the neighbors, everyone who knew her—the meal should be a celebration of Meat's life."

I could tell that Dad really liked this idea. It was the same tone he used when he told people about Multicultural Day at the Unitarian Church.

Then my sister said, "I'm not eating it. I'm a vegetarian."

"Oh, good one," said Dad. He tried to laugh, to turn her words into a joke. No one else laughed.

"I'm serious," my sister said, so coldly it froze everyone else.

We drove several miles before Dad tried to say anything else.

"You know, we've got nothing to apologize for," he said. "We gave her a good life. Much better than any factory farm animal's."

Mom still hadn't said a word.

My sister shook her head. "This whole family's screwed

up," she muttered, and kicked the sole of her foot against the dashboard. Dad opened his mouth to scold her, but he wasn't used to doing the scolding, and he turned his head toward Mom. But she was looking out the window, with her jaw clenched tight. That's when I started to cry.

"Shut up!" I yelled at my sister. "You weren't even nice to her!" If my seat belt had let me, I would have reached around and punched her.

"How are you better?" my sister shouted back. "Be nice to her then kill her? I never pretended. The rest of you are phonies!"

That made Dad so angry, he pulled the car over to the side of the road. "That's enough!"

I was hysterically crying by now, and I couldn't pay much attention to what he and my sister were yelling at each other. Mom pulled me into her lap and stroked my hair. If she said anything, I don't remember it now.

◈

It was a few weeks before I was over it. There had been all that blood, gushing out of her throat and onto the floor in two streams. I dreamt about it over and over, and I asked a lot of questions about what happens when you die. I couldn't shake the look, either, on Meat's face right before the butcher stunned her, and the way her eyes fixed on me while she hung there in the killing room. Did she hate me? I wondered. Mom told me no, Meat couldn't hate me. "You took care of her and played with her when no one else wanted to," Mom said in a sad voice. Maybe Mom was sorry she hadn't been nicer.

I got a little better after we ate her. The first dinner was just me, Dad, and Mom, not a big party like Dad had first wanted. My sister wouldn't come out of her room, but Dad winked and said that was fine, more for us. He made a little toast to Meat and thanked her for her life and said we were glad to know her. Which was all true. After my first bite, with the tender flesh practically melting on my tongue, I thought Dad was right—something you raise yourself always tastes better. Anyway, Meat tasted better than all the other meat I'd eaten before—or since, to be honest. We gave some of the cuts to the neighbors who were interested and froze the rest for special occasions.

I started to worry less that she hated me and that we'd done something terrible by killing her. After all, every piece of meat was a live thing once. But I still missed her. When I got home from school, my first instinct was to look for her in the yard, and I even called her name a few times, forgetting she wasn't there to hear. Everywhere I went in the neighborhood felt lonely because last time I'd been there with her. Mom and Dad tried to spend more time with me, but they were both busy with work and chores and the civic associations that Dad signed up for.

Things didn't really get better again until my eighth birthday. That's when we got Drumstick.

Aren't You Pretty?

Patrick Hicks

I never wanted kids. I was happy with my single life in my single home with my single meals because it was no fuss—just me and my animal companions. Every night I'd come home from my job at the animal shelter, feed the dogs, maybe drop a cricket into Bessie's terrarium. Then I'd watch a PBS documentary about tree frogs, or maybe I'd put in a movie like *Born Free* or *Never Cry Wolf*. It was a gentle life of my own making. No husband. No kids. Just me and my little zoo.

One night in December, the phone rang, and as I reached through the dark I knew it was bad news—calls at 1:32 in the morning are fattened upon evil—but what I heard made me sit up and pucker.

"Your brother's house is on fire."

The cuckoo clock in the dining room ticktocked its wooden heartbeat. Sheba put her wet nose against my wrist, which gave me a little jolt.

"Andi," the voice said. "Did you hear me? Your brother's house is on fire. You best come over here pronto."

I don't remember leaving the house or starting my Jeep

or opening the garage door, but I do remember traveling through snowy streets and worrying about hitting a stray dog. Wet, heavy flakes flowed into my headlights, and when I came to a stoplight I gripped the steering wheel and tried to calm myself. I blew into my shaking hands and wondered if I'd heard the message correctly.

Then I saw the smoke. A thick, black paste that tarred the sky, it roared froth and choked the moon, rising up from Creek Street. My heart thumped between my breasts as I ran the red light, thinking: *What if Sara's in there?* I sped down slick streets, murmuring the thought as if it were a mantra.

Big yellow trucks and police cars blocked the road, and their emergency lights bounced off windows, an epilepsy of color. I parked a block away from my brother's house, which was already greased with fire. Boiling flames winged out from the house, making the air wavy. I ran down the street in my slippers and pushed through a crowd of winter coats. I stood there, stunned, and felt clumps of snow melt down my ankles. I wanted to scream Sara's name, but a spreading tower of black awed me into silence. I put my hands on the back of my head and looked at the gigantic crackle and crash of the house, how the moon shimmered in the waving heat, how this lovely home was being eaten alive as if by a wild animal. Snorting sparks popped up, up, up. A firefighter moved past me and spoke into a radio. He ran into the backyard, leaving sooty footprints behind in the snow.

Then I saw my brother, Steve, on his knees near the front door, holding a cell phone with both hands.

"Where's Sara?" I yelled as I approached him.

He ignored me, so I cupped his face. The stubble on his cheeks felt like a cat's tongue, all gritty and warm, and as I spoke again I enunciated every word.

"Where. Is. My. Niece."

"I've been trying to call her."

"Is she at a sleepover somewhere else? Oh, thank God." I wrapped my arms around him and began to weep with joy. The tears felt good on my cheeks. "She's safe," I breathed into his ear. "Safe."

But Steve pointed to the house as fire spun into the sky. The Christmas lights on the gutter were still blinking as if nothing were wrong, and a sign on the garage door winked out the words *Ho Ho Ho* even as firefighters clacked more ladders off their trucks.

"She's in *there?*"

He seemed confused. "She won't answer her phone. These things cost hundreds of dollars, and I thought it'd keep her safe. Why doesn't she answer her phone?"

Steve looked at me with tears streaming down his face. Firelight danced on his skin, and the wet in his eyes were full of flame. His bottom lip quivered.

A firefighter jogged up and lifted a plastic shield from his face. He had a scar on his forehead and spoke quickly. "You the mother?" he asked me.

"No, the aunt. The mother's gone."

He grabbed my elbow and pushed me toward a canary-yellow truck, one that had axes and chainsaws inside. The engine idled up as water from a hose rained down onto the house. Little crystals of water froze in midair. The stink of burning wood and plastic filled up the night as smoke geysered into the air. It was dark, like used motor oil, and granular ash swirled around the house.

The firefighter paid no attention to any of this. He took off his helmet, nodded toward Steve, and said, "That guy's in shock, but I need to know where—"

A rubber band snapped inside me, and the words came fast. "She's only eight, for Christ's sake! Get her out of there! *Do* something!"

"Where's her room?"

"There!" My finger stabbed the air.

We looked at the front door as a stained glass window burst into twinkling color. I heard a roar, like a jet taking off, and looked at the sky because I couldn't believe something that loud had come from inside the house. A wave of heat pushed me back, and that's when I thought of Sara, huddled on the floor, her lungs bloody with superheated smoke.

I ran for the front door. My vision blurred, and I felt myself come out of my body. I wanted to throw my body into the flames and trade myself for her. It would be a simple sacrifice. Me for her.

I screamed her name until my chest hurt and I was panting. Hands grabbed my shoulders, and I slid cartoonishly on the snow before a fireman pushed me to the ground.

Men in heavy reflective gear and oxygen tanks gathered near the mailbox as crystallized water tinkled around them as if they were in some kind of strange snow globe. Somewhere overhead a helicopter shredded the night, and a person next to me yelled out that it must be an air ambulance from Saint Paul. Amid so many pulsing lights and distractions, my whole being concentrated on the front door. It was a doorway to hell—all fire and sucking black—and the Christmas lights around it began to melt in droplets of colorful flame. *Ho Ho Ho* still flashed on the garage door, and each word was bright behind a veil of smoke.

Something limp was brought out of the house, and the firefighters ran past me, their oxygen masks clicking on and off like scuba divers'. My mind was so polluted with fear that I kept looking at the front door, expecting Sara to walk out in her nightgown and maybe cough a few times, but, as the paramedics began to put tubes into what looked like a burnt, rolled-up rug, I came to understand that this scorched little thing was my niece.

She was covered in soot, and I thought she might be okay

when they hosed her off—just get a rag and clean her up. The air filled up with the smell of licorice, and I heard a sizzling, crackling sound. I would later learn this was the stink and the sound of Sara's burning skin. I had to close my eyes and block out the world for a moment. I took a deep breath. I counted to five.

My niece's face was swollen, and her right cheek was cooked to the bone. Most of her hair was matted in clumps, and I wondered about her mouth because her lips were little sausages. How on earth would she ever smile again? How on earth would she recognize herself in a mirror?

My brother came up and covered his own mouth. Emergency lights flickered on his face.

"You the father?" a paramedic asked.

"That's not my daughter. That's not Sara."

"Sir ... "

"That's not my daughter. What is that?"

Another firefighter put a gloved hand on Steve's shoulder and guided him to the ambulance. He clicked the seat belt into place, and I heard him say, "Go easy, man. Go easy."

Images of hurt animals flickered through my mind—cats, rabbits, hamsters, dogs, snakes—people could be so awful to beautiful things, and it made me yell at my brother as I slapped the ambulance door with my palm. "What have you done?"

A firefighter wrapped his arms around my waist, but I continued to shriek as the ambulance pulled away. "What have you done?"

The ambulance rounded the corner, and the helicopter thudded toward County Road 5. There, on a deserted winter road, my niece would be transferred from one emergency vehicle to another. A hospital in Saint Paul was already prepping an operating room, and I felt a burst of joy that technology might save her.

Hoses waved jets of water onto the house as vinyl siding dripped like candle wax onto concrete. I marched to my Jeep and slammed the door so hard the frame rocked back and forth.

As I pulled away from the emergency lights, fat snowflakes drifted into my headlights. I sped up, wondering if Sara was still alive and wondering how on earth the fire had started. The helicopter lifted into the night. Its pulsing red light thumped away.

◆

She was an American Wirehair, and if I focused on her tail it was easy to believe she was still whole and unhurt. But if I looked at her head—my God. Why would a bunch of thugs hold down a cat and stuff a firecracker in her ear? What kind of little monster lights that firecracker, then runs away giggling with his friends? It's the giggling that gets to me as I snap on antiseptic gloves and move toward this beautiful cat. We named her Moonlight because that's what saved her: a full moon. Had it been dark out, she never would have been found near that drainage ditch. Never.

This is a familiar story at rescue shelters across the nation. I've seen dogs strung up and beaten; I've seen rabbits with their ears scissored off; I've seen ferrets blowtorched in their cages and turtles used as baseballs. People are so cruel I don't believe in human kindness anymore. Moonlight may be missing an ear, and much of her head is just lumpy scar tissue now, but she purrs when I touch her. She sticks out her tongue when I lean into her good ear and whisper, "Aren't you a beautiful little creature? Aren't you pretty?"

The purple skin makes me think of Sara and how I'd gotten to the hospital thirty minutes after the helicopter did.

Steve smelled of wood smoke and was playing with his cell phone as I ran into the waiting room.

"She's still not answering her phone," he said, obviously still in shock.

My brother has always loved gadgets. I've seen him give Sara the best computer or the latest zippy toy, and I've seen him walk away as if his fatherly duty was over. He once bought her a motorized scooter (no helmet) and then disappeared to watch a football game on his fifty-inch TV. Although I've never understood my brother, there was something in his voice that night, something terrified as we waited outside the burn unit. When the doctor told us Sara was stable, Steve didn't look up. He just played with his cell phone—opening it, closing it—as Dr. Wong talked about burnt collagen, reticular fibers, and nerve endings.

"She's sedated," Dr. Wong said, leaning forward. "But you can't see her. Not yet. When you *do* see her, prepare yourself. Don't gasp or make her feel bad. Just walk in and treat her normal. Understand?"

Steve nodded and looked at his boots, discolored and stained with road salt. After a long pause, he said, "I didn't leave her in the house, you know. I woke up to all this smoke and I stumbled around choking and looking for her and I thought maybe she was outside, so I go outside and I look but she's not in the front yard or the backyard. That's when the fire guys show up, and they won't let me back in the house."

Dr. Wong closed her eyes and nodded. "I'm sorry. Truly."

Steve stood up, paused on wobbly legs, and walked away as if he'd heard none of it. His footsteps echoed down the tiled hallway, and I heard the elevator ping open. I worried he was going to abandon Sara as her mother had four years earlier. She'd gone out for yet another wild evening of booze and had never come home. She'd called from Las Vegas to say she wanted a life with "some adventure." When I tried calling her, she never answered her phone.

And now, a week after the fire, Steve wasn't answering his damn phone either.

Moonlight purred as I stroked her back. "Aren't you beautiful? Aren't you pretty?"

The phone rang down the hall, and it kept on ringing because the new girl was at lunch. A few dogs in the back began to yodel, so I walked over and picked up the receiver with two fingers. The smell of antiseptic glove was strong in my nose. "Animal Rescue."

"You guys sell dogs?"

"Not over Christmas."

"But I want a puppy for my daughter."

I put the phone into my shoulder and snapped off a glove. "Like I said, we don't place our animals over Christmas. Check back in January."

"But she wants a puppy."

"Animals aren't toys. You want a toy, go to the mall."

"But that's not why—"

"Look. Too many animals get hurt over the holidays. Owning a pet means growing up and being responsible. You can't bring life into your home and ignore it because you want to do other things like watch football on TV."

I slammed down the phone and, to my deep surprise, began to sob.

◈

The fluorescent lights and the smell of bleach in the burn unit reminded me of the animal shelter. Multicolored lines were painted on the floor, zooming off down the hallway, sometimes zagging around corners. Nurses walked around in green smocks and laughed near vending machines full of junk food. This was my seventh trip in three days, and I was beginning to recognize their faces. Mandy was the head nurse; she had big brown eyes and used her hands a lot when she talked. Her ponytail flapped back and forth as she walked over to me.

"Andi. How you doing? Talk to me."

I shrugged a shoulder. "Has my brother showed up yet?"

"No, but a present was delivered this afternoon."

My eyes narrowed. "What kind of present?"

She put a clipboard under her arm and pretended to hold something heavy. "It's a huge basket of flowers. *Eee*-normous."

At the nurses' station was a gigantic wicker basket with sunflowers and daffodils; a teddy bear held a box of chocolates, and a chain of plastic hearts dangled from the basket's handle. A greeting card the size of a book was propped open, the words *Get Well Soon* in huge, glittering letters. The words *From Daddy* were printed in the corner by some computer.

I touched one of the plastic hearts and wondered if I could trace where it was sent from.

Mandy backed toward the door and opened it with her rump. "The kiddo is still on ketamine and Versed. One drug numbs the pain, and the other affects memory so she's not afraid of treatment. We don't want her to remember the debriding process because we'd never get her back into that whirlpool if she did. I tell you what though … the kiddo is tough. A trooper." A pause. "She's been asking for you."

Visiting the burn unit demanded a whole new language of me. Ativan, Silvadene, bacitracin, Flexinet, autograft, xenograft. Debriding. That was the worst word of all. Debriding happened when they lowered Sara into a whirlpool twice a day and scrubbed her clean. The bubbling water became a soup of dead skin, and they used tiny knives to flay her body. The pain made her scream at first; then she passed out. The first time I saw this, it didn't look as if skin was peeling off her at all because it was a whitish-tan mush floating in the water. It looked like thinned oatmeal.

Mandy gave me a surgical gown, and I tried to put it on quickly, to show her I knew what I was doing, but my fingers were clumsy.

"The kiddo's full of grit and—turn around. I'll tie that for you. Here's a mask and some gloves. Like I was saying, she's a trooper, that niece of yours. Even adults break down in that whirlpool. They say it's like bathing in a tub of hot acid."

I scrubbed my hands with green foam and looked at the door to Sara's room. Nothing went in there that wasn't sanitized first—even toys had to be bleached, and it made me wonder how I'd ever get my house clean enough for Sara. Dog and cat hair were everywhere, but she couldn't live with all those germs. If Steve didn't appear soon, a choice would have to be made between Sara and my pets. I felt a little ball of red-hot anger glow in my chest. I imagined slapping my brother across the face.

"Any idea how the fire started?" Mandy asked. Her voice was chipper. Too chipper.

"The fire department says it was an Advent candle that wasn't blown out. Happens all the time around Christmas, apparently. It's no one's fault." I swallowed and hated hearing those words spill out of my mouth. "But it feels like it should be *someone's* fault, you know? It's hard not to blame my brother. He fell asleep in front of the TV."

"Oh." Mandy lowered her head as if weighing what to say next. "Why did he run away?"

Rusty wire filled my veins, and I found myself saying things I probably shouldn't have, but it felt good to unload.

"He's always been afraid of responsibility. He's just a big stupid kid, always liked things, gadgets, more than people. For all I know, he's in some bar right now, sipping whiskey. Someplace where time has stopped and no one asks him any questions. Someplace where he can go numb."

In a flash, my mind went back to that moment four years ago when he showed up at my house with Sara. She wore a puffy winter coat and held a stuffed animal, a huge fluffy dog clutched to her heart. That's how I knew Sara's mother had skipped town. Steve told me he was going to look for her. At the time he gave me some cockamamie story about checking hotels up near Duluth where they sometimes went to play slots, and he dropped a pink backpack at my feet.

"I'll be back in a few hours. I gots to check something out."

Without waiting for my response, he walked down the wooden stairs of my porch and got into his new silver BMW. Where he got the money for it, I never learned. Sara looked at the ground, as if none of this surprised her in the least, and I held up my hand as if to call him back. But the engine revved, and he left in a growl of noise. A cloud of exhaust hung in the crisp winter air. It wisped away, ghostlike.

I'd looked down at Sara, knowing my day was shot. "So, you want some mac and cheese?"

She didn't look up.

"There's a new cat inside," I said, shifting my weight.

"What happened to *this* one?"

"Never you mind. She's better now, and that's all that matters."

Steve returned three weeks later. *Three weeks*. And with a different car, one with Nevada license plates. He walked into my house, thanked me with a bottle of champagne, and gave his daughter a bear hug as if nothing was wrong.

"Hey, sweet pea," he said, brushing hair out of her eyes. "Let's go home."

The memory of this must have made my face go sour because Mandy put up her gloved hands as if to say she was sorry to have asked such a personal question. And then, after a long moment of silence, she told me about other burn victims. She did this, I think, to make me feel better, as if to say that others have had it bad, too, and I wasn't alone. Mandy told me about farmers with electrical burns and kids who pulled coffee pots down onto their heads and fast-food workers who tripped hands first into deep fat fryers.

Again Mandy used her rump to open the last door into the burn unit. "Follow me," she said.

A steam bath surrounded us, and I felt my hair follicles open up in the muggy heat. The room was a sauna because it helped soothe the blowtorching pain that clung to Sara's body. Burn victims say the pain of regenerating skin feels as if they are still caught in a room of flame—as if they are still on fire, still burning.

A turban of gauze covered Sara's head, and her lips were little purple slugs. She looked wet and leathery, as if her skin were made of cling film, and her eyes were closed in a drugged-dreamy-nevercare snoozing. I wanted to wrap my arms around her, I wanted to press all of my love into her, I wanted to put my hands on her face and kiss her forehead and bring her into my chest—but of course I could do none of these things. The most basic human impulse is to gather someone in your arms and tell them they'll be okay, but I couldn't do this.

My eyes filled with tears even as my heart boiled with hate. *How could he leave?*

Mandy leaned over the bed. "Sara? Honey? Your aunt's here."

The little girl began to whimper. Then she began to yowl.

◈

I stomped snow off my boots while Sheba and Luna

twirled on the carpet like dervishes. They barked and nuzzled into me, which made me feel I was really home. I got a glass of zinfandel and slumped into the sofa. Miss Emma sunned herself on a patch of carpet while, inside her warm terrarium, Bessie hunched over the husk of a cricket. Her spinnerets massaged out a messy web. Every living thing in my house was happy, safe.

That's when I tried calling Steve again. I knew he probably wouldn't answer, but I just had to say the words that were bubbling in my head. I had been practicing the speech all the way home and I was ready. Primed.

His phone rang once, twice, three times. It went to voice mail.

"Hey. It's me. Don't you think you should be here with your daughter? What kind of monster walks away from a damaged little girl when she needs him most?" My voice softened, and I picked dog hair from my trousers. "Look, if you came home now she probably wouldn't even realize you left her again. She's so drugged up she doesn't know what's happening. Don't be a jerk, Steve. Your daughter needs you. Just come home. Okay? Please?"

I touched the off button and took a long pull of zinfandel. As I swallowed, I heard the delicate bones in my ears pop. It was such a small thing, but it suddenly seemed so grand and important. Such a forgettable moment of daily biology, but yet it was so precious, so easy to take for granted.

Snow drifted past the window in fat flakes, and I took another sip. A plastic Santa was on the roof of a neighbor's house, and I imagined him sliding down the chimney with a sack full of toys. I closed my eyes and saw Sara opening box after box of healthy skin. I saw her put on skin grafts as if they were T-shirts and panties and socks and gloves and leotards. She would clothe herself in new flesh, and not a scar would be on her. On a bright Christmas morning she would stand naked before a full-length mirror, and then my niece—this little girl with a lifetime of world ahead of her—would dance around the house. She would walk into the family room, raise her arms to somersault across the floor, and she would be whole again. Made new. Given a second chance.

Miss Emma jumped onto my lap and mewed with an arched back. I'd rescued her when a family moved across the country and left her in a garbage can. I looked around at my collection of the saved. Sheba and Luna. Reggie and Trouble. Joey. Sphinx. Bessie in her terrarium—soon she would be shedding her skin; soon she would push into the world as a whole new tarantula. I poured another glass of zinfandel, liking my little life. No husband. No kids. Just me and my little zoo.

My body floated away on the wine, and I leaned back into the couch. The house around me felt warm and calm. Tranquil. The furnace clicked on, and a soft exhale of heat from one of the registers flapped against my trouser leg. I thought of Moonlight and knew I'd bring her home soon. I'd need more cat food and probably another litter box. Squeaky toys, too. How could I make the spare bedroom more cozy for her?

I tried calling my brother again. His phone rang and rang until—

"Hello? Steve?"

◈

I hadn't been to the house since the fire and, in my head, I imagined the bottom floor might be blackened with smoke, the front door might have a Do Not Enter sign on it, and maybe, just maybe, a few shingles were burnt. What I expected was very sanitized and orderly. But fire doesn't work that way. It eats everything in its path. It devours.

The house looked like the burnt ribcage of some prehistoric animal. Nothing was left. It was all charcoal bones—gutted and useless. Snow had drifted into what used to be the family room, and the smell of extinguished bonfire was everywhere. The whole house was ringed with a moat of frozen, ashy water. A lump in my throat made my chin quiver, and that's when all of these unwanted memories came rushing back. The emergency lights. The roar. The screaming. The burnt rug that was brought outside. That sizzling, crackling sound.

I sniffed and cleaned up some twigs. Gathering things helped focus my mind, and that's when I noticed a neighbor had cleared the sidewalk with his snow blower. Such a simple thing to do, such a wonderful act of kindness. The tears returned, and I looked up at the leaden sky. I sniffed a few more times and bit my lip.

"God damn it," I said to no one in particular.

I wandered in a daze and searched for anything that might be salvaged. A plastic sled was melted into the chain link fence and, impossibly, a snowman looked at the disaster in mild surprise; his scarf flapped in the wind, and footprints from a thousand firefighters danced around him.

I turned from the charcoaled world of death and tried to remember Thanksgivings and birthdays in this house, but the smell of creosote and cinders filled up my nose. I turned away and thought of Sara in high school and wondered who on earth would take her to prom. How would she be treated? She needed someone to champion her and stand next to her as she walked down a path that was forever scorched with burn tissue. This house fire had been branded onto her skin. The past was tattooed deep into her flesh. Decades of gawking strangers waited up ahead for her.

Right then I flipped open my phone and called him. I expected to leave a message, but what I heard made my blood turn to slush. *The number you have reached has been disconnected … The number you have reached has been disconnected … The number you have reached has been disconnected …*

I shut my phone and looked at the ruined house. Snow began to tumble from the sky, and it got caught in my hair. A few flakes hit my eyelashes, and I blinked them away.

◈

A red line on the floor zigzagged me through the hospital, and when I got to the familiar swinging doors I reached for a surgical gown. My fingers tied it behind my back, and I snapped on some antiseptic gloves.

"I'm ready," I said.

Mandy was with me again, and she entered the burn unit rump first, as usual, to keep her hands free and sterile. I stepped into the muggy heat of the steam room. It smelled of lotion, gauze, and pus. Sara was propped in bed, her left arm exposed. It was a mass of lilac scar tissue. Large bits of black were flaking off, and she looked shiny, as if she had just come out of a womb. She leaked platelet-rich plasma.

Debriding was so painful, so torturous, and yet it had to be done. Little bits of herself were flayed off every morning, and at night her body knitted new patches of wet skin together. She was shedding dead skin cells for new skin cells, regenerating herself into a new being. In this way she would become whole again. I thought of Moonlight and all the bandages I'd put on her scorched little head. I also thought of Bessie crawling out of her molt as a new spider.

I couldn't hug my niece, and I wanted to hug her. I wanted to gather her into my arms and rock her like a baby. I wanted to absorb all the pain, gather up all the wounding emotions, and I wanted to give her a normal life. More than anything else, I wanted to bring her home.

My hand hovered above her charred purple skin. I pretended to caress her arm. I stroked the air, inches above her wrist, and she opened her eyes. They were blue and frightened.

I bent into her good ear. "Aren't you beautiful," I whispered. "Aren't you pretty?"

The Ecstatic Cry

Midge Raymond

One of our gentoo chicks is missing.

I flip through our field notebook to find Thom's chart of the colony, then match nest to nest. According to our records, the chick was two weeks old, but now the rocky nest is empty, the adult penguins gone. I search but find no body; its disappearance must have been the work of a predatory skua. When skuas swoop down to snatch chicks or eggs, they leave little behind.

I move away from the colony and sit on a rock to make some notes. That's when I hear it—a distinctly human yelp, and a thick noise that I have heard only once in my life and have never forgotten: the sound of bone hitting something solid.

I stand up and see a man lying in the snow, a red-jacketed tourist from the M/S *Royal Albatross*, which dropped its anchor in our bay this morning. He'd fallen hard, landing on his back and apparently narrowly missing a gentoo, which is now scurrying away. The man doesn't move.

I hold still for a moment, hoping he will get up. When I

see a spot of red spreading in the snow underneath his head, I start toward him.

Fifteen other tourists are within thirty yards, yet no one else seems to notice. They're still up the hill, listening to their ship's naturalist, the whirs and blips of their digital cameras obscuring all other sounds on the island.

But my research partner, Thom, must have seen something; he gets to the man first. And now a woman is scrambling guardedly down the same hill, taking care, despite her hurry, to avoid the same fate.

I turn my attention to the man. His blood is an unwelcome sight, bright and thin amid the ubiquitous dark-pink guano of the penguins, and replete with new bacteria, which could be deadly for the birds. I stifle an urge to start cleaning it up.

Thom's voice snatches back my attention. "Deb," he says sharply, glancing up. He'd spent two years in medical school before turning to marine biology, and he looks uncharacteristically nervous. By now, four more tourists in their matching red jackets have gathered around us, and I can see that Thom wants to shield them from what he sees.

I hold out my arms and move forward, forcing the red jackets back a couple of steps. The woman who'd hurried down the hill is trying to see past me. She looks younger than the usual middle-aged passengers who cruise down to Antarctica, the ones who have already been everywhere else, who want to check off their seventh continent. "Are you with him?" I ask her. "Where's your guide?"

"No—I don't know," she stutters. Blonde hair trails from under her hat into her eyes, wide with an anxiety I can't place. "He's up there, maybe." She motions toward the gentoo colony. I glance up. The hill has nearly disappeared in fog.

"Someone needs to find him," I say. "And we need the doctor from the boat. Who's he traveling with?"

"His wife, I think," someone answers.

I kneel next to Thom, who's examining the man's head. If we were anywhere but Antarctica, the injury may not seem as critical. But we are at the bottom of the world, days away from the nearest city, even farther from the nearest trauma center. There is, of course, a doctor along on the cruise, and basic medical facilities at Palmer Station, half an hour away by boat—but it's not yet clear whether that will be enough.

The man hasn't moved since he fell. A deep gash on the back of his head has bled through the thick wad of gauze that Thom has applied. Voices approach—the guide, the wife, the doctor. The man's chest suddenly begins heaving, and Thom quickly reaches out and turns his head so he will vomit into the snow. More bacteria.

The man shudders and tries to sit up, then loses consciousness again. Thom presses fresh gauze to his head.

"What happened?" the wife cries.

"He slipped," I tell her.

Thom and I move aside for the doctor.

"How could this happen?" the wife wails. It's no mystery, I want to tell her; her husband is about sixty pounds overweight and can't see his own feet, which are stuffed into cheap boots despite the fact that he paid thousands of dollars for the tour that brought him here. But I silently place a hand on her shoulder as crew members show up with a gurney. "We need to get him to Palmer," the doctor says, her voice low. The man remains still.

Thom helps them load him onto the gurney, and they take him to a Zodiac. I get a plastic bag from our camp, then return to the scene and begin scooping up the blood- and vomit-covered snow. Because we're in one of the last pristine environments in the world, we go to great lengths to protect the animals from anything foreign. Visitors sterilize their boots before setting foot on the island, and again when they depart. No one leaves without everything they came with.

Yet sometimes, like now, it seems pointless. Injuries like this are unusual, but I've seen tourists drop used tissues and gum wrappers, not knowing or caring enough to pick them up. I want to chase after them, to show them our data, to tell them how much the fate of penguins has changed as more and more tourists pass through these islands. But Thom and I must be patient with this red-jacketed species—we are employed by the same tour company that brings them here. The company sponsors our research, and in turn it gets a tax break and two more experts to give on-board lectures and slide shows. With government dollars harder and harder to come by, I'm grateful—but we earn it more each season, and our work often takes a backseat to keeping the tourists happy.

Thom returns and stands over me, watching for a moment. Then he says, "They need me to go to Palmer with them."

I look up. "Why?"

"The crew is crazed," he says, "and they need someone to stay with the victim and his wife."

"I guess we're at their mercy." I inspect the ground to make sure there's nothing left in the snow. Thom doesn't have a choice—we're often asked to fill in for the crew—but I know what he is really asking me. We have been partners for three years, and I've never spent a night on this island alone.

I stand up. Thom is short, and I'm tall, so we look each other directly in the eye. "Go ahead. I'll be all right."

"You sure?"

"I'll keep the radio on, just in case. But yeah, I'll be fine. After all this, I'll enjoy the peace."

"I'll be back tomorrow," he says.

We go back to camp, a trio of tents a few yards off the bay. From there we can watch the ships approach and, more important, depart.

Another Zodiac is waiting to take Thom to Palmer. He grabs a few things from his tent and gives my shoulder a squeeze before he leaves. "I'll buzz you later," he says. He smiles, and I feel a sudden, sharp loneliness, like an intake of cold air.

I watch the Zodiac disappear around the outer cliffs of the bay, then turn back to our empty camp.

◈

It's hard to believe on an evening like this, with the air sogged with rain and the penguins splashing in a pool of slush nearby, that Antarctica is the biggest desert in the world, the driest place on earth. The Dry Valleys have not seen rain for millions of years, and thanks to the cold, nothing rots or decays. Even up here, on the peninsula, I've seen hundred-year-old seal carcasses in perfect condition, and abandoned whaling stations frozen in time. Those who perish in Antarctica—penguins, seals, explorers—are immortalized, the ice preserving life in the moment of death.

But for all that stays the same here, Antarctica is constantly changing. Every year, the continent doubles in size as the ocean freezes around it; the ice shelf shifts; glaciers calve off. Whales once hunted are now protected; krill once ignored are now trawled; land once desolate now sees thousands of tourists a season. But it remains, to me, a place of illusion; when I'm here, I still feel comfortably isolated, even though increasingly I am not.

I make myself a cold, unappetizing supper of leftover pasta and think of my return, two weeks away. Thom and I will be eating well then, cozily aboard the *Royal Albatross* with its gourmet meals and full bar. And my sense of aloneness will be gone, replaced with lectures and slide shows and endless Q&A sessions.

I finish my supper and clean up, careful not to leave even

the smallest crumbs behind. At nearly ten o'clock, it's still bright outside, the sun still hours away from its temporary disappearance. I take a walk, heading up toward the colony that was so heavily trafficked today, the one the man visited before he fell. The empty nest remains deserted. The other penguins are still active, bringing rocks back to fortify their nests, feeding their chicks. Some are sitting on eggs; others are returning from the sea to reunite with their mates, greeting one another with a call of recognition, a high-pitched rattling squawk.

I sit down on a rock, about fifteen feet away from the nearest nest, and watch the birds amble up the trail from the water. They appear to ignore me, but I know this isn't true; I know that their heart rates increase when I walk past, that they move faster when I'm around. Thom and I are studying the two largest penguin colonies here, tracking their numbers and rates of reproduction, to gauge the effects of tourism and human contact. Our island is one of the most frequently visited spots in Antarctica, and our data shows that the birds have noticed. They're experiencing symptoms of stress: lower birth rates, fewer fledging chicks. It's a strange irony that the hands that feed our research are the same hands that guide the boats here every season, and I sometimes wonder what will happen when the results of our study are published.

Often when I watch the penguins, I forget I'm a scientist. I become so mesmerized by the sounds of their purrs and squawks, by the precision of their clumsy waddle, that I forget that I have another life, somewhere else—that I have an apartment in Eugene, that I teach marine biology at the University of Oregon, that I'm forty-two years old and not yet on a tenure track, that I haven't had a real date in three years. I forget that my life now is only as good as my next grant, and that, when the money dries up, I'm afraid I will, too.

I first came to Antarctica when I was thirty, to study the

emperor penguins at McMurdo. I've been returning every season I can, to whatever site I can, by whatever means. Thom and I have two seasons left in our study. He's married, with two small kids at home; this will be it for him. I'm still looking for another way to make it back.

What I'd like most is to return to the Ross Sea, to the emperors. This is the species that captivates me—the only Antarctic bird that breeds in winter, right on the ice. Emperors don't build nests; they live entirely on fast ice and in the water, never setting foot on solid land. I love that during breeding season, the female lays her egg, then scoots it over to the male and takes off, traveling a hundred miles across the frozen ocean to open water and swimming away to forage for food. She comes back when she's fat and ready to feed her chick.

My mother, still hopeful about marriage and grandkids for her only daughter, says that this is my problem, that I think like an emperor. I expect a man to sit tight and wait patiently while I disappear across the ice. I don't build nests.

When the female emperor returns, she uses a signature call to find her partner. Reunited, the two move in close and bob their heads toward each other, shoulder to shoulder in an armless hug, raising their beaks in what we call the ecstatic cry. Penguins are romantics. Most mate for life.

◈

In the summer, Antarctic sunsets last forever. They surrender not to darkness but to an overnight dusk, a grayish light that dims around midnight. As I prepare to turn in, I hear the splatter of penguins bathing in their slush, the barely perceptible pat of their webbed feet on the rocks.

Inside my tent, I extinguish my lamp and set a flashlight nearby, turning over a few times to find a comfortable angle.

The rocks are ice-cold, the padding under my sleeping bag far too thin. When I finally put my head down, I hear a loud splash. It was clearly made by something much larger than a penguin—yet the ship is long gone. And when you're alone in Antarctica, you are truly alone.

Feeling suddenly uneasy, I turn on my lamp again. I grab my flashlight and a jacket and hurry outside, toward the rocky beach.

I can see a shape in the water, but it's bulky and oddly shaped, not smooth and sleek, like a seal. I shine my flashlight on it and see only red.

It's a man, in his cruise-issued parka, submerged in the water up to his waist. He looks into the glare of my flashlight. I stand there, too stunned to move.

Then the man turns away, and he takes another step into the water. *He's crazy*, I think. *Why would he go in deeper?* Sometimes the seasick medication that tourists take causes odd and even troubling behavior, but I've never witnessed anything like this. As I watch him anxiously from the shore, I think of Ernest Shackleton—of his choices, the decisions he made at every step to save the lives of his crew. His decision to abandon the *Endurance* in the Weddell Sea, to set out across the frozen water in search of land, to separate his crew from one another, to take a twenty-two-foot rescue boat across eight hundred miles of open sea. I also think of Robert Scott, leading his team to their deaths just as his competitor became the first to reach the South Pole—and of the expedition guides who last year drove a Zodiac underneath the arc of a floating iceberg, only to have the berg calve and flip their boat, drowning the driver. In Antarctica, every decision is weighty, every outcome either a tragedy or a miracle.

Now, it seems, my own moment has come. It would be unthinkable to stand here and watch this man drown, but attempting a rescue could be even more dangerous. I'm alone.

I'm wearing socks and a light jacket. The water is freezing or a few degrees above, and though I'm five-nine and strong, this man is big enough to pull me under if he wanted to, or if he panicked.

Perhaps Shackleton only believed he had options. Here, genuine options are few.

As I enter the icy water, my feet numb within seconds. The man is now in up to his chest, and by the time I reach him, he's thoroughly disoriented. He doesn't resist when I clutch his arms, pulling them over my shoulders and turning us toward the shore. In the water he is almost a dead weight, but I feel a slight momentum behind me as I drag him toward the beach. Our progress is slow. Once on land, he's near collapse, and it takes all my strength to heave him up the rocks and into Thom's tent.

He crumples on the tent floor, and I strip off his parka, boots, and socks. Water spills over Thom's sleeping bag and onto his books. "Take off your clothes," I say, turning to rummage through Thom's things. I toss him a pair of sweatpants, the only thing of Thom's that will stretch to fit his tall frame, and two pairs of thick socks. I also find a couple of T-shirts and an oversized sweater. When I turn back to him, the man has put on the sweats and is feebly attempting the socks. His hands are shaking so badly he can hardly command them. Impatiently, I reach over to help, yanking the socks onto his feet.

"What the hell were you thinking?" I demand, not really expecting an answer. I hardly look at him as I take off his shirt and help him squeeze into Thom's sweater. I turn on a battery-powered blanket and unzip Thom's sleeping bag. "Get in," I say. "You need to warm up."

His whole body shudders. He climbs in and pulls the blanket up to cover his shoulders.

"What are you doing here?" I ask. I, too, am shaking from

the cold. "What the hell happened?"

He lifts his eyes, briefly. "The boat—it left me behind."

"That's impossible." I stare at him, but he won't look at me. "The *Royal Albatross* always does head counts. No one's ever been left behind."

He shrugs. "Until now."

I think about the chaos of earlier that day. It's conceivable that this stranger could have slipped through the cracks. And it would be just my luck.

"I'm calling Palmer. Someone will have to come out to take you back." I rise to my knees, eager to go first to my tent for dry clothes, then to the supply tent, where we keep the radio.

I feel his hand on my arm. "Do you have to do that just yet?" He smiles, awkwardly, his teeth knocking together. "It's just that—I've been here so long already, and I'm not ready to face the ship. It's embarrassing, to be honest with you."

"Don't you have someone who knows you're missing?" I regard him for the first time as a man, rather than an alien in my world. His face is pale and clammy, its lines suggesting he is my age or older, perhaps in his late forties. I glance down to look for a wedding band, but his fingers are bare. Following my gaze, he tucks his hands under the blanket. Then he shakes his head. "I'm traveling alone."

"Have you taken any medication? For seasickness?"

"No," he says. "I don't get seasick."

"Well," I say, "your boat's probably miles away by now, and we need to get you on it before it goes any farther."

He looks at me directly for the first time. "Don't," he says.

I'm still kneeling on the floor of the tent. "What do you think?" I ask. "That you can just stay here? That no one will figure out you're missing?"

He doesn't answer. "Look," I tell him, "it was an accident. No one's going to blame you for getting left behind."

"It wasn't an accident," he says. "I saw that other guy fall.

I watched everything. I knew that if I stayed they wouldn't notice me missing."

I stand up. "I'll be right back."

He reaches up and grasps my wrist so fast I don't have time to pull away. I'm surprised by how quickly his strength has come back. I ease back down to my knees, and he loosens his grip. He looks at me through tired, heavy eyes—a silent plea. He's not scary, I realize then, but scared.

"In another month," I tell him, as gently as I can manage, "the ocean will freeze solid, and so will everything else, including you."

"What about you?"

"In a couple weeks, I'm leaving, too. Everyone leaves."

"Even the penguins?" The question, spoken through clattering teeth, lends him an innocence that almost makes me forgive his intrusions.

"Yes," I say. "Even they go north."

He doesn't respond, and I stand up. He lets me leave, and I go straight to the radio in our supply tent, hardly thinking about my wet clothes. Just as I'm contacting Palmer, I realize that I don't know his name. I go back and poke my head inside. "Dennis Singleton," he says.

The dispatcher at Palmer tells me that they'll pick up Dennis in the morning, when they bring Thom back. "Unless it's an emergency," he says. "Everything okay?"

I want to tell him it's not okay, that this man might be crazy, dangerous, sick. But I can't exaggerate without risking never being taken seriously again—too big a risk with two more seasons of research here. So I say, "We're fine. Tell Thom we'll see him in the morning."

I return to the tent. Dennis has not moved. He is staring at a spot in the corner, and he barely acknowledges me.

His quietness is unsettling. "What were you doing in the water?" I ask.

"Thought I'd try to catch up to the boat," he says.

"Very funny. I'm serious."

He doesn't reply. A moment later, he asks, "What are *you* doing here?"

"Research, obviously."

"I know," he says. "But you'd have to be a real loner to enjoy being down here." He rubs the fingers of his left hand. Thinking of frostbite, and a change of subject, I grab his hand to examine his fingers. "Where do they hurt?"

"It's not that," he says.

"Then what?"

He hesitates. "I dropped my ring," he says. "My wedding band."

"Where? In the water?"

He nods.

"For God's sake." I duck out of the tent before he can stop me. I hear his voice behind me, asking me where I'm going, and I shout back, "Stay there."

I rush toward the water's edge, shivering in my still-damp clothes. The penguins purr as I go past, and a few of them scatter. I shine my flashlight down to the rocks at the bottom. I follow what I think was his path into the water, sweeping the flashlight back and forth in front of me.

I'm in up to my knees when I see it—a flash of gold against the slate-colored rocks. I reach in, the water up to my shoulder, so cold it feels as if my arm will snap off and sink.

I manage to grasp the ring with fingers that now barely move, then shuffle back to shore on leaden feet. I hobble back to my own tent, where I strip off my clothes and don as many dry things as I can grab. My skin is moist and wrinkled from being wet for so long. I hear a noise and look up to see Dennis, with the blanket still wrapped around his shoulders, crouched at the opening to my tent.

"What are you staring at?" I snap. Then I look down

to what he sees—a thin, faded T-shirt, no bra, my nipples pressing against the fabric, my arm flushed red from the cold. I pull his ring off my thumb, where I'd put it so it wouldn't fall again, and throw it at him.

He picks it up, holding it but not putting it on. "I wish you'd just left it," he says, almost to himself.

"A penguin could have choked on it," I say. "But no one ever thinks about that. We're all tourists here, you know. This is their home, not ours."

"I'm sorry," he says. "What can I do?"

I shake my head. He can't leave, which is the only thing I want him to do. There's nowhere for him to go.

He comes in and sits down, then pulls the blanket off his shoulders and places it around mine. He finds a fleece pullover in a pile of clothing and wraps it around my reddened arm.

"How cold is that water, anyway?" he asks.

"About thirty-five degrees, give or take." I watch him carefully.

"How long can someone survive in there?"

"A matter of minutes, usually," I say, remembering the expedition guide who'd drowned. He'd been trapped under the flipped Zodiac for only a few moments but had lost consciousness, with rescuers only a hundred yards away. "You go into shock," I explain. "It's too cold to swim, even to breathe."

He unwraps my arm. "Does it feel better?"

"A little." Pain prickles my skin from the inside, somewhere deep down, and I feel an ache stemming from my bones. "You still haven't told me what you were doing out there."

Setting his ring to one side, he reaches over and begins massaging my arm. I'm not sure I want him to, but I know the warmth, the circulation, is good. "Like I said, I lost my ring."

"You were out much farther than where I found your ring."

"I must have missed it." He doesn't look at me as he

speaks. I watch his fingers on my arm, and I am reminded of the night before, when only Thom and I were here, and Thom had helped me wash my hair. The feel of his hands on my scalp, on my neck, had run through my entire body, tightening into a coil of desire that never fully vanished. But nothing has ever happened between Thom and me, other than unconsummated rituals, generally toward the end of our stays. After a while, touch becomes necessary, and we begin doing things for each other—he'll braid my long hair; I'll rub his feet.

Suddenly I pull away. I regard the stranger in my tent: his dark hair, streaked with silver; his sad, heavy eyes; his ringless hands, still outstretched.

"What's the matter?" he asks.

"Nothing."

"I was just trying to help." The tent's small lamp casts deep shadows under his eyes. "I'm sorry," he says. "I don't mean to cause you any trouble. I know you don't want me here."

Something in his voice softens the knot in my chest. I sigh. "I'm just not a people person, that's all."

For the first time, he smiles, barely. "I can see why you come here. Talk about getting away from it all."

"At least I leave when I'm supposed to," I say, offering a tiny smile of my own.

He glances down at Thom's clothing, pulled tight across his body. "So when do I have to leave?" he asks.

"They'll be here in the morning."

Then he says, "How's he doing? The guy who fell?"

It takes me a moment to realize what he's talking about. "I don't know," I confess. "I forgot to ask."

He leans forward, then whispers, "I know something about him."

"What's that?"

"He was messing around with that blonde woman," he says. "The one who was right there when it happened."

"How do you know?"

"I saw them. They had a rendezvous every night, on the deck, after his wife went to bed. The blonde was traveling with her sister. They even ate lunch together once, the four of them. The wife had no idea."

This is the type of story I normally can't tolerate, but I find myself intrigued. "Do you think they planned it?" I ask. "Or did they just meet, on the boat?"

"I don't know."

I look away, disappointed. "She seemed too young. For him."

"You didn't see her hands," he says. "My wife taught me that. You always know a woman's age by her hands. She may have had the face of a thirty-five-year-old, but she had the hands of a fifty-year-old."

"If you're married, why are you traveling alone?"

He pauses. "Long story."

"Well, we've got all night," I say.

"She decided not to come," he says.

"Why?"

"She left, a month ago. She's living with someone else."

"Oh." I don't know what more to say. Dennis is quiet, and I make another trip to the supply tent, returning with a six-pack of beer. His tired eyes brighten a bit.

He drinks before speaking again. "She was seeing him for a long time," he says, "but I think it was this trip that set her off. She didn't want to spend three weeks on a boat with me, without him."

"I'm sorry." A moment later, I ask, "Do you have kids?"

He nods. "Twin girls, in college. They don't call home much. I don't know if she's told them or not."

"Why did you decide to come anyway?"

"This trip was for our anniversary." He turns his head and

gives me a cheerless half-smile. "Pathetic, isn't it?"

I roll my beer slowly between my hands. "How did you lose the ring?"

"The ring?" He looks startled. "It fell off during the landing, I guess."

"It was thirty degrees today. Weren't you wearing gloves?"

"I guess I wasn't."

I look at him, knowing there is more and that neither of us wants to acknowledge it. And then he lowers his gaze to my arm. "How does it feel?" he asks.

"It's okay."

"Let me work on it some more." He begins to rub my arm again. This time, he slips his fingers inside the sleeves of my T-shirt, and the sudden heat on my skin seems to heighten my other senses: I hear the murmur of the penguins, feel the wind rippling the tent. At the same time, it's all drowned out by the feel of his hands.

I lean back and pull him with me until his head hovers just above mine. The lines sculpting his face look deeper in the tent's shadowy light, and his lazy eyelids lift as if to see me more clearly. He blinks, slowly, languidly, as I imagine he might touch me, and in the next moment he does.

I hear a pair of gentoos outside, their rattling voices rising above the night's ambient sound. Inside, Dennis and I move under and around our clothing, our own voices muted, whispered, breathless, and in the sudden humid heat of the tent we've recognized each other in the same way, by instinct, and, as with the birds, it's all we know.

◈

During the Antarctic Night, tens of thousands of male emperors huddle together through a month of total darkness, in temperatures reaching seventy degrees below zero, as they incubate their eggs. By the time the females return to the colony, four months after they left, the males have lost half their body weight. They are near starvation, and yet they wait. It's what they're programmed to do.

Dennis does not wait for me. I wake up alone in my tent, the gray light of dawn nudging my eyelids. When I look at my watch, I see that it's later than I thought.

Outside, I glance around for Dennis, but he's not in camp. I make coffee, washing Thom's cup for him to use. I drink my own coffee without waiting for him; it's the only thing to warm me this morning, with him gone and the sun so well hidden.

I sip slowly, steam rising from my cup, and take in the moonscape around me: the edgy rocks, the mirrored water, ice sculptures rising above the pack ice—I could be on another planet. Yet for the first time in years, I feel as if I've reconnected with the world in some way, as if I am not as lost as I've believed all this time.

I hear the sound of a distant motor and stand up. Then it stops. I listen, hearing agitated voices—it must be Thom, coming from Palmer, having engine trouble. He is still outside the bay, out of sight, so I wait, washing my coffee mug and straightening up. When the engine starts up again, I turn back toward the bay. A few minutes later, Thom comes up from the beach with one of the electricians from Palmer, a young guy named Andy. I wave them over.

They walk hesitantly, and when they get closer, I recognize the look on Thom's face. Even before he opens his mouth, I know, with an icy certainty, where Dennis is.

"We found a body, Deb," he says. "In the bay." He exchanges a glance with Andy. "We just pulled him in."

I stare at their questioning faces. "He was here all night," I say. "I thought he just went for a walk, or—" I stop.

Then I start toward the bay.

Thom steps in front of me. He holds both of my arms. “There’s no need to do this,” he says.

But I have to see for myself. I pull away and run toward the water’s edge. The body lies across the rocks. I recognize Thom’s sweater, stretched over Dennis’s large frame.

I walk over to him. I want to take his pulse, to feel his heartbeat. But then I see his face, a bluish white, frozen in an expression I don’t recognize, and I can’t go any closer.

I feel Thom come up behind me. “It’s him,” I say. “I gave him your sweater.”

He puts an arm around my shoulder. “What do you think happened?” he asks, but he knows as well as I do. There is no current here, no way to be swept off this beach and pulled out to sea. The Southern Ocean is not violent here, but it is merciless nonetheless.

◈

Antarctica is not a country; it is governed by an international treaty whose rules apply almost solely to the environment. There are no police, no firefighters, no medical examiners. We have to do everything ourselves, and I shrug Thom off when he tries to absolve me from our duties. I help them lift Dennis into the Zodiac, the weight of his body entirely different now. I keep a hand on his chest as we back out of the bay and speed away, as if he might suddenly try to sit up. When we arrive at Palmer, I finally give in, leaving others to the task of packing his body for its long journey home.

They offer me a hot shower and a meal. As Andy walks me down the hall toward the dormitory, he tries in vain to find something to say. I’m silent, not helping him. Eventually he updates me on the injured man. "He's going to be okay," he tells me. "But you know what's strange? He doesn't remember anything about the trip. He knows his wife, knows who the president is, how to add two and two—but he doesn't know how he got here, or why he even came to Antarctica. Spooky, huh?"

He won't remember the woman he was fooling around with, I think. *She will remember him, but for him, she's already gone.*

◈

Back at camp, I watch for the gentoos who lost their chick, but they do not return. Their nest remains abandoned, and other penguins steal their rocks.

Ten days later, Thom and I break camp and ready ourselves for the weeklong journey back. We have been working in a companionable near-silence, which is not entirely unusual. Our weeks together at the bottom of the earth have taught us the rhythms of each other's moods, and we don't always need to talk. We do not talk about Dennis.

Once on the boat, the distractions are many, and the hours and days disappear in seminars and lectures. The next thing I know, we are a day away from the Drake Passage, the last leg of our journey, where the Southern Ocean, the Pacific Ocean, and the Atlantic all meet and toss boats around like toys. The tourists will get sick, and I will take as much meclizine as I can stomach and stay in bed.

But today I wander around the ship, walking the halls Dennis walked, sitting where he must have sat, standing where he may have stood. I'm with a new group of passengers now, none of whom would have crossed his path. A sleety rain begins to fall, and I go out to the upper deck. As we float through a labyrinth of icebergs, I play with Dennis's wedding ring, which he'd left on the floor of my tent. I wear it on my thumb, as I did when I'd first found it, because that's where it fits.

Because of the rain, I'm alone on the deck when I see it—a lone emperor penguin, sitting atop an enormous tabular iceberg. A good field guide would announce this sighting on the PA—the passengers aren't likely to get another chance to see an emperor. But I don't move; I watch her as she preens her feathers, and I imagine that she is feeling leisurely, safe, in a moment of peace she can't comprehend or enjoy.

They aren't aware of it, but the emperors' very survival depends on all but perfect timing. During the breeding season, the female must return from her journey within ten days of her chick's hatching. If she doesn't show, her partner, nearly dead from starvation, has no choice but to abandon their chick. He can't get beyond his own instinctual will to live.

I believe that penguins mourn. I've seen Adélies wander their colonies, searching for mates that never return; I've seen chinstraps sitting dejected on empty nests. And I've seen the emperors grieve. The female returns, searching, her head poised for the ecstatic cry. When her calls go unanswered, she will lower her beak to the icy ground, where she will eventually find her chick, frozen in death, and she will assume the hunched posture of sorrow as she wanders across the ice.

Litter

Philip Armstrong

The rain has fallen steadily all week. Most of each day you've spent dozing, whole mornings and into the afternoons, huddled in a side-door in an alley, roused every few minutes by a damp gust. The wind brings smells gathered by rain from the air and from sidewalks and gutters: wet cardboard, sodden leaves, meat scraps, dog and cat and human piss, liquefied exhaust fumes, seepage from the decaying rat that blocks the drain upstream.

It's late afternoon when you raise your head. The dim light is getting dimmer. You prick your ears. At least you prick the left ear and the stump where the right one used to be. You yawn and lick your lips. Inhale. The wet air has a steamy taint. Boilers are firing up for the night ahead, which means the stores are closing soon. You uncurl your rib-marked body, get to your feet and slowly stretch, back legs, front legs. You shake all over, shrugging your winter coat into place. You squat to pee on a pile of crushed pizza boxes, trot out of the alley and into the street. Follow your nose.

The burger places smell best, but they deliver least, so

you pass them without pausing, though your nostrils take in their empty promises. You thread your way among the crowds hurrying home. You sidestep fancy crossbreeds on leashes and the outstretched paws of toddlers. At the tree by the bus stop you put your nose to work. Your nostrils figure out who's passed by and how often and how long ago, and what each one has eaten recently, and who is sick and who is well, and who's randy and who's not interested. Before moving on you leave a dribbled message of your own.

It's dark now, and the stores are shut. Their twilit windows are blurry in the drizzle. You weave past shopping bags and raincoats, dodge skateboarders, hop over puddles. Reaching a corner, you turn left and left again, slip between two facades. You come out in a square space, an empty shaft walled by the backs of buildings. Among the Dumpsters and stacks of broken pallets there are barrels holding scraps from a diner. You insert your long nose under a lid and flip it off.

◈

It was this time last year you met your most recent human companions. You were hanging round the glass doors of the big building on the corner. Late each night dozens of people emerge from here and toss things in the curbside trash can before they walk off. The can's always too full, and the new stuff falls to the sidewalk, and you snaffle it, little slices and pods of taste: corny, salty, creamy, sweet.

That night, you were licking up a spilt ice-cream when you saw a couple stop to watch you. Arm-in-arm, they watched as you licked the sidewalk clean and crunched the cone. You raised your head and looked at them, ready to retreat. The man crouched and whistled and held out his hand.

You turned your head to go, but something landed on the

asphalt next to you, and you gave a little skip of fright. The man had thrown something, a sweet brown pod. Cautiously you advanced. It smelt good, and you ate it and looked back at him. He was still down on his haunches with his arm stretched out, and in his hand was another sweet brown pod.

You looked at the pod and then up at the man's eyes. And you and he understood the same thing: that when he and the woman turned and walked home, you'd follow.

◈

It didn't take long to get used to being round humans again, or living in a house. Your body soon recalled what you'd known as a pup, your hackles smoothing under his hands, your jaws and ears loosening under his fingers.

The man's scent had dark tones, authority in his sweat and a bite of something else, something you couldn't get clear. Yet to you he was soft-spoken and soft-bodied. Polite. He never touched without signaling his intentions. Most times he'd just hold out a hand and wait. When you pinned back your ears and slunk forward, he caressed your head or scratched the base of your tail. Within a week or two, you came whenever he asked.

The woman was stiffer, pricklier, more scary. She put your back up with her jittery movements and the slow-leak nerviness from her pores.

You were allowed in the house till the man and woman were ready for bed. Then he took you to a kennel in the backyard. More comfortable than you were used to, but all the same you felt more vigilant than ever. Not because of the new surroundings—you were used to new surroundings—but because you no longer had only yourself to look out for.

The first night you slept with eyes half open and both ears

up. You woke before dawn and stretched and squatted to pee. The golden cord of urine, warm and fragrant, joined you to the new ground, made it familiar. Squatting a second time you felt the pulse of a turd curve out of you, smelt the damp dirt curving up. You dug your feet in the earth and threw clods backwards, mingling the smells of soil and shit.

You opened your nose to the day. Particles of morning air mixed with particles lining your nostrils. Odor became flesh. Your ears and eyes strained into the growing light. You felt barks rising inside you, rushing from your chest and throat in response to this new place, these new companions and the new day. You opened your mouth and let them fly—deep, loud barks, a dozen, two dozen, two dozen more, great flocks of them.

Lights went on next door. More barks rose up in you, and you let them out. A window opened, someone shouted, and you barked some more. After a bit you heard a fist pound at the front door of your house, and voices rose in argument. You had to bark louder, more urgently.

A door slammed; footfalls pounded through the house. The back door opened. As the man came near, you lowered your ears and curled your tail between your thighs.

But all he did was bend down and scratch your head. He was laughing. He repeated that sound he always used on you.

◈

In that house, mornings were best. Each day the man put a big plate of biscuits by the back door. After licking the last crumbs you'd lay under the kitchen window where the sunlight warmed the floor. With your chin on the tiles you moved only your eyes, following the man and woman as they poured cereal and drank coffee and toasted toast. You liked the shuffle of their bare feet on the floor and the smell of their just-awake breath.

One morning after breakfast, when the man and the woman went to wash and dress, you approached the white oblong in the kitchen corner. You'd watched them opening and closing it many times, felt the cold mist from it that carried smells of meat and butter and milk. Now your nose flipped the door open. You chewed up a packet of meat cylinders and a sticky-skinned dish of salty rashers. You lifted out a tub of yellow grease and stamped on it till it opened and licked it clean, and did the same to three pots of milky jelly. You were sniffing a spilt bottle of red stuff when the kitchen door opened. The woman stood there. She started to snarl, and you backed away. Then the man appeared and barked, but not at you. The woman fell quiet, and the man turned to you and laughed and made his sound for you.

◈

Most of each day you spent in the backyard, waiting for the man to come home. He'd come out to see you straight away, and you'd greet him every way you knew how. Then he'd put a leash on your collar, and the three of you—the man, the woman, and you—would go down the street to the park. You figured out how to walk at the man's side because the leash yanked your throat if you didn't. The woman walked behind.

As soon as the leash came off, you'd race over to the peach tree. First time you came here there'd been a cat in the branches, so after that you had to check each time. Finding nothing, you'd nose along the weeds and dirt by the fence. Your puff-sniffs created eddies of dust to carry odors into the openings and out of the side-slits in your nostrils.

At the corner of the fence you'd turn and race back to the man. Unless a scent caught you and stopped you short, turned you back, made you quest from side to side, seeking the invisible point where you crossed its path.

Sometimes the man tried throwing sticks. But you never liked to fetch. Also you didn't like it because each time the man raised his hand to throw a stick, the woman flinched. A tiny movement. Imperceptible, but you perceived it.

It's early morning, and the rain has stopped. Something's going on. You feel a gut-tremble and a teat-tightening, a back-end buzz. Your limbs are more limber than usual. Your ears are in on the act, too. Right now you can make out two dozen different footfalls, ten coattails flapping in the wind, seventeen voices speaking in five buildings. You can tell the relative distances and speeds of two buses several streets away. A cat leaps to the top of a fence, and you hear it catch its breath when it spots you.

You set off to the creek. Your nostrils are going all out. It's easy to navigate the odor map of streets and backyards and empty lots. Now and then you locate something too good to resist—a long-dead bird or some seepage from a pile of pick-and-mix detritus—so you drop a shoulder and roll. You browse on a few dead grass stems, retching as they tickle your throat, to clear your senses for the next thing.

You make your way to the culvert under the bridge. That's where the kids in hoodies gather. They sniff fumes that make you sneeze, but they also leave all kinds of scavenge. Today, though, you find something you don't expect. One of your own kind, but not quite the same. When he approaches, you smell him smelling you. At first you fear he might be a bully. But then you realize he's actually the answer to your heightened senses.

He isn't the best specimen you've ever known, but he's in the right place at the right time, so you present yourself, and he's keen enough. You enjoy it so much you clamp on for twenty minutes before letting him go, and he yelps and scampers off.

◈

Your life in that house ended suddenly one evening. The man and the woman were sitting in front of the flickering, buzzing box in the corner, as they did most evenings. The woman sat on the other side of the room from the man, and you lay at his feet. The shapes on the screen, without smell or vibration, meant nothing to you. Instead you listened to the rats chirping in the wall and dozed.

But then you woke suddenly, all senses alert. You wondered what was up. The man and woman were bickering, their voices harsh. That was normal; they did it most nights. But tonight there was something else on its way. You could smell something different in the formula of the man's sweat, hear the prickle of hairs rising on the woman's neck. Silently you slid behind the couch.

The voices got louder over the next half hour and stopped only when the beating began. Through your belly, pressed against the wooden floor, you felt it, blow by blow.

When it was over the woman lay sobbing. The man threw himself on the couch, breathing heavily. He made the sound he kept specially for you, the sound that meant you should go to him.

But instead of an answering surge in your muscles that would pull you to your feet and walk you in his direction, your bladder and bowels opened. Their warm smell filled the room.

Cursing, the man threw the end of the couch from the wall and seized you by the scruff. You turned your head, inserted your right canine in his arm, and ran it down to his wrist, opening a long gash, bone-deep. With a yell he let go, and you scrambled into the next room and under the table.

The smell of the man's blood spread all around as he ran to the kitchen and rattled through drawers. The woman was pleading and sobbing from the other room.

Through chair legs you watched him approach. He overturned the table, and, before you could get away, he threw the leash around your neck and pulled it tight. Clamping your head between his knees, he bent down. In his hand was the blade that you'd often watched him use to slice your meat. The cut took only an instant, but you heard each fiber of flesh as it parted. Then you could hear nothing on that side but a muffled confusion, and where the ear had been you felt a burning trickle.

The other ear heard something though: the opening door and sounds from outside. The woman had slipped behind the man, and she stood holding the front door wide. Her eyes met yours.

Convulsively you slipped the man's hold and pulled your wounded head out of the leash. A moment later you were through the door and on the street. From behind came more shouting.

You paused a moment, looked back. The man stood on the porch in the yellow light. Blood flowed freely from his arm. He called out to you roughly.

The woman appeared behind him with a towel and started wrapping it around his wound. Then she held his injured arm in hers and drew him back inside. She didn't look back at you. The door closed.

You shook your head and gave a yelp of pain. Then started running along the street, through the rain.

Today you wake even hungrier than usual. Your belly is swelling fast, and it itches and aches as though little muzzles are questing inside, this way and that. Your litter will come at the wrong time. If you can't find enough food you'll have to eat them, at least the weaker ones.

It's too early to forage, so for now there's nothing to do but curl up in your doorway and return to sleep. After stretching and shaking you turn three times to lie down. Within moments your eyelids sag and your paws twitch and your nostrils dilate and protrude, giving out little puffs.

You dream of running through a world without earth or sky, a void except for floating globes of smell, which gently fall and burst on you. Your skin opens to receive them. Pores or nostrils appear and disappear wherever the smell-bubbles meet your body, the way surface water opens and closes under drops of rain.

The Boto's Child

Rosalie Loewen

I knew the truth from the beginning although I did not always believe it. It is amazing, the mind's ability to bend the truth to serve the heart.

It was our honeymoon. Matt was a graduate student, three years into a ten-year Ph.D. Unable to find work in my field, I had abandoned my own undergraduate biology degree and was idling in an interminable office manager position. Our marriage came after a long relationship: an acquiescence on his part, a gambit on mine. I was seeking transformation. Of course, we both knew that his studies came first.

Manaus wasn't much of a honeymoon, despite the exotic locale. Matt had a grant to study the piraiba fish of the Amazon: giant catfish, ancient monsters, longer than a man and wider than you could put your arms around. There weren't many of the piraiba left then, and for all I know they are gone now. Ashes to ashes, mud to mud, same as the rest of us.

Matt's contact at the Manaus university arranged our

hotel and found us a three-day riverboat excursion for the locals' price on the Rio Negro, the Black River.

The Black River. A spidery line on the map belies its voluptuous curves and doglegs forming a loose plait that refuses to answer to the cartographer. Born thin and icy in the Andes, it streams down from Colombia along the lip of Venezuela, gathering water and richness as it wallows into the colossal bowl of the Amazon basin. There it reaches full strength, covering even the tallest kapok trees at a whim, leaving them suspended underwater, their leaves still moving gently in remembrance of breezes. Finally, turbulent and treacherous with rips, its broad back furrowed and peaked white, it slams into the Amazon River. Even there, it holds its own, a solid black line cutting out and into the milky chocolate of the Amazon for miles before finally roiling under and into that great river and allowing itself to be carried to the sea.

Our excursion boat was peeling white with green trim, damp-soft with rot in the corners, a clumsy oval of two wedding cake tiers covered by a peaked wooden awning. Under the awning, there was room either for two hammocks or a table and two chairs. This top deck was for us, the tourists, while the lower deck had hammocks for the crew, a glass-windowed steering house, a corner of a kitchen, and trapdoor access to the big diesel motor, the heart that beat beneath the deck.

We boarded the boat at 10:00 a.m., in deference to our photocopied itineraries, and then sat under the awning in the smog-choked harbor watching other tourist boats, nearly identical to our own, take on their passengers. Each boat had a similar version of our crew: the bellied, beetle-browed captain and the thick-armed female cook, missing a random assortment of teeth between them; and the guide who, in a sea of ubiquitous flip-flops, sported immaculate sneakers as his badge of prestige.

On that first morning underway, I sat beneath the awning on the top of the boat as we pulled away from the docks, carefully keeping my winter-pale limbs in the safety of the shade. Matt buried himself in his field guide, cracking the new spine with practiced fingers, light brown hair falling over a brow already grown higher since we'd met our freshman year.

I had hoped, although I knew better, that when we married he would see me again, really see me, and that it would be the way it had been when we first met: how he used to search for me in a room and that mild electric shock when his arm brushed mine. If he would look at me again, I thought I would be able to catch a glimpse of myself. If he would want me, I could want myself. Just by the way he opened that book, I already knew that it had been a mistake, that it wouldn't happen.

I could not stand the thought of reading. The close-pressed verdure of the shore shimmering in the heat, the swirling tea-colored water, and the noxious throb of the engine hypnotized me. With the sun almost directly overhead, I let go of all sense of direction, watched the vultures circle, and let the pulsing chant of the jungle saturate my brain.

In the evening, after motoring through the day, we anchored in a quiet lagoon, so tranquil and beguiling that I could not understand why all the other tourist boats weren't anchored there as well. Later, I discovered that it was simply the satin quality of the evening air that gave this illusion of perfection; it was the same miracle in every lagoon on every evening.

A strong caipirinha, the raw sting of the liquor sugared smooth, quieted the leftover hum that ran through my body even after the engine ceased. The deck rocked soothingly with the motion of the cook preparing dinner below. When I closed my eyes, the solidity of the boat beneath me disappeared, and I was suspended in water turned air.

The people of the Amazon sleep in hammocks their whole lives, hanging above snakes, spiders, errant flooding, and more insidious microscopic threats. Not being accustomed, I found it difficult to sleep this way. I loved the first part, how in the moment between wake and sleep I could feel the slippery motion of the earth turning beneath me. But I could not stay asleep; I longed to turn on my side, to bury my face in a pillow. I supposed one could get used to it. My new husband, for example, snoring next to me with the field guide open across his chest, sweat-smeared glasses still perched on his nose. Not much honey in this honeymoon, after all. It is a mystery to me how babies could be conceived in a hammock.

Mid-morning on the second day we motored to a long rickety dock that ended in a series of haphazard stairs, the boards gone gray and splintery. A lean, barefoot man dressed in faded gym shorts and a pink shirt that might once have been red came to the end of the dock, his eyes shaded by a jaunty, albeit ragged, fedora. He caught the rope that our captain threw and tied us down. "Nature walk," our guide stated and stepped onto the dock, where a knot of dirty, mostly naked children materialized to tug at his pockets.

To the children's delight, he swung his nylon backpack off his shoulder and began to distribute slices of cheap white sandwich bread, one to each child. They crowed and crammed the bread into their mouths so that their hands would be free to beg for more. Relenting, enjoying their antics, the guide handed out all the slices until the bread was gone. The children snatched the plastic bag out of his hands and threw it into the water, where it floated forlornly in the wash from our boat.

My attention was caught by the man in the hat who was, at that moment, handing up to the kitchen window a string of small flat fish, gleaming and still rainbow-shined. Piranhas. I thought of their glass-slivered teeth and steel-sprung jaws.

It was the man in the fedora who led the way during our nature walk, cutting the vines away with his machete, our guide two steps behind him. I sensed that it was he and not the guide who was knowledgeable about the mysteries of this place, who was keeping us safe. He smiled shyly when introduced to us, revealing small, almost pointed teeth, but did not speak. He did not take any food when we stopped for our picnic: packets of saltines, individually wrapped squares of sticky pink jellied guava, and slices of a crumbly salty white cheese. The guide's backpack held a small, crinkly bottle of water for each of us, but he handed the man a can of beer that the man opened immediately and drank as though it were water.

The jungle is a great deceiver. From afar it seems lush, ripe, dripping with fruit juice and honey. But as we passed through a green curtain into the shadowed interior, I felt uneasy, menaced. A vine frilled with purple passiflora trailed us into the darkness, each blossom an ornately spiked and poisoned beauty, the crown of an evil queen who casts her sleeping spell. The fleshy red fingers of the birds of paradise cupped offerings of fetid dew and drowned insects. When the guide lopped off a section of the noosed vines dangling overhead to show us fresh water inside, I was horrified to see the vine recoil and spring away from his machete, as though it were alive.

One lesson of the jungle is this: It is the small things that are the most dangerous. Forget the jaguars and the crocodiles—a gem-like frog smaller than a child's fist is so poisonous that simply touching it is lethal. There is a tiny ant fearsome enough that the local natives endure its bite as the ultimate test of manhood, just as African warriors might hunt a lion. Don't lean up against any trees, the guide warned us, pointing out a slender palm with spines as long as my pinky finger. When we finally ducked out into the daylight again, I squinted with relief as though the lights had come back up in a theater at the end of a horror movie.

Although it was well into the afternoon, the equatorial sun was still strong enough to prick at my skin like a tattoo needle. The guide assured us we could safely swim, and to coax us into the water he put on his own swim shorts and dove off the dock. He and Matt, sharing a set of plastic swimming goggles, soon began comparing notes on various strands of greenery they pulled up from the bottom. Matt seemed fearless in the water, despite, or perhaps because of, his knowledge of the antediluvian leviathans and other threats that lurked beneath. Sometimes the ones who know are less afraid than the ones who have no idea.

That evening, the meal was delicious; the small fish passed up to the cook earlier in the day reappeared, pan-fried. Their flesh was as sweet as marmalade and pulled easily away from the bones and the crisp, salty skin. The whole of the little fish that I had been served hardly amounted to three forkfuls, and I asked the cook for another helping. She laughed as she served me; then she blushed and said it was *pr'amor* as she ducked away. I looked to the guide, who explained that the local people believe that eating piranha is an aphrodisiac.

After dinner, while Matt sat at the table under the awning looking through his books and penning careful notes into the margins, I walked to the open part of the deck. The blue was fading from the sky to the east, and broad bands of citrus colors in the west reflected in the still waters. I could hear the cook rattling dishes in the pocket-sized galley below me, rinsing the remnants of canned green beans and dozens of needle-sharp bones into the forgiving waters of the river.

Then, along the horizon, a dark band like a storm cloud rapidly approached the boat. In a moment I was surrounded by thousands of swallows. My ears were filled with the rushing, whispered clap of their wings as they flew by, long sweeping tails lending grace to their hurried purpose. The wind of their passage lifted the air around me, stirred my hair. Then they thinned, passed by, and were gone.

I glanced back at Matt, but it seemed he had not looked up from his work. When I leaned over the balcony I could see the top of the cook's head leaning out of her window, watching in the direction where the birds had receded. I felt the desire to keep this to myself, not to tell anyone. This was meant for me, meant to mark me.

That night, lying in my hammock, I could feel the heat rising up within me as the swaying of the boat released butterflies into my stomach. A strange energy ran in a low hum throughout my body. Suddenly it was torture to remain in the hammock for a moment more. Perhaps the cook had been right about the piranhas.

Matt was already asleep, mouth slack, breath thick. I swung out of my hammock, slid into my flip-flops, and came out from under the awning, seeking respite from myself. The reflection of a full moon made the water brighter than the sky.

I climbed down from the boat, sat on the edge of the dock, and dipped my feet into the water. I thought for an instant about the piranhas as my toes and shins became ghostly beneath the water. There was no fear this time; the eaters had been eaten.

The river was a degree warmer than the air, velvety on my skin. Little wavelets stroked my legs. I felt such relief from the touch of the water that in a moment I had pulled off my cotton shirt and shorts and slid in with a small splash.

I heard quiet footsteps on the dock. He stopped near my clothes, his profile and the fedora clearly outlined against the deep blue of the night sky. I held my breath, frozen in the water. I did not feel embarrassed, only uncertain.

He smiled then, his teeth showing white for a moment in the dark. Turning to the water he whistled, soft and high, paused, listened, and whistled again. He looked out over the water, seeing something I could not.

He lowered himself into the water. As he went in he gracefully swept the fedora from his head and left it on the dock before slipping completely under. He surfaced again, close to me. I tensed and filled my lungs, prepared to kick or scream. Holding up his hand to me, palm out, in a universal gesture meaning *pause, peace, silence, wait*, he looked out over the water again and clicked his tongue against his teeth.

I turned to look. Soon a long, slender snout poked out of the water, followed by a blunt, bulbous forehead, the sleek, rosy-colored skin fading to blue and silver under the light of the moon. Immediately I knew from the travel brochures that this was the pink dolphin, the boto. The pictures showed smiling, bikini-clad tourists in sunlit lagoons offering fish to the boto. The boto approached me slowly, butted its long beak against my hand, and then lolled on its side. As though in a dream, I placed my hand gently on the skin. It was cool and smooth, slippery, firm.

The dolphin lay still under my hand and then, in a quick motion, flicked away to swim around me in tight circles, brushing against me, bumping gently into me underwater. I grasped hold of the short fin, and with a surge the dolphin pulled me forward. I lost my grip, surprised by the power and strength of the creature. I could see the roll and curve of the surface where the dolphin turned and came back to me. The dolphin twined through my legs like an oversized cat, pushing me through the water, lifting me. The ecstasy of the moment squeezed the breath from my chest.

All too soon, the dolphin swam away. The ripples left in its wake smoothed and drifted outward. I stilled my breath to listen, but there was nothing except the night sounds of the insects and frogs, a wild trilling, an insistent and strident proclamation of their existence.

I thought of the man then and turned a slow circle to find him in the water, but there was no sign. His fedora still rested near my clothes, and the dock was dry. Suddenly I felt chilled and exhausted. I swam back to the dock and pulled myself out. I dressed quickly, and the material clung and twisted on my wet skin. I looked for the man again, along the banks, but the night air had grown murky, wisps of cloud wreathing the moon, and I could not see where he might have left the water. I left his hat on the dock and returned to my hammock, where I swayed so quickly into sleep that I hardly remembered lying back.

I was still tired in the morning but relaxed, a thousand tiny splinters of worry worn to smoothness by the passage of water. I stayed in my hammock, even as I felt the quake of the engine starting, and heard voices call back and forth. I let the light filter rosy through my eyelids and the hum of the day rise up around me.

We spent the day chugging back to the city docks, and I watched the jungle change: Patches of grass began to grow where the trees had been cut back, and a few single, modest shacks appeared, leaning to one side or the other, their doorways black rectangles. Then the houses began to group themselves and straighten up; doors appeared in doorways and screens on windows. The water took on a greasy sheen, and the tea color muddied as though cream were being stirred in.

Back in Manaus in the evening, we disembarked. We shook the captain's hand and offered cash tips to the captain and the cook, with a larger tip for the guide, whose shoes were still, somehow, spotless. Before we could turn away, the cook suddenly reached out and patted my cheek with a stained and calloused hand. With a half smile she spoke to me, and I turned to the guide for translation.

"She says, '*sorte, alegria, e lagrimas.*' That means luck,

happiness, and tears. I think it is some kind of saying for your marriage or for your honeymoon." Under the gaze of the cook, her brown eyes webbed with red, I felt my cheeks grow hot. I thought then that she must have seen me slip naked into the water, seen the boto come to me.

Although our hotel was simple—thin mattresses over sagging springs and cracked porcelain in the bathroom—it seemed a luxury to be able to shut the door and have the floorboards stay in one place. Matt headed immediately for the shower, but I was reluctant to wash the smell of the river water off my skin. I combed my hair, found a clean sundress at the bottom of the suitcase, and put it on, fresh cotton soft against bare skin. The room, with its painted concrete walls, held the cool of the earth despite the polluted humidity of the city outside.

The hotel clerk pointed us to a restaurant down the street for dinner. The heavy scent of fish flesh in hot oil sank toward the floor, with a tang of vinegar floating over the top. A waiter welcomed us in; handed us greasy, laminated menus; and brought us to a rickety table circled by plastic chairs. In fair English he rattled off a list of the fish that were available today: tambaqui, surubim, jaraqui. Clearly the menu was only a formality. He recommended pirarucu, which was, he added gravely, "very good for luck." I let Matt do the ordering for both of us.

The wait for our orders was long and allowed us to cycle through an overpriced drinks menu. We ordered cachaça mixed with local fruits and gritty with sugar. We tried it with fruta do conde, pulpy and musty-sweet, and then with cashew fruit juice, which left an odd dry feeling on my tongue, a hint of the caustic sap that feeds the fruit. The sides of the drink were decorated with carambolas sliced into stars, somehow unripe, perfectly ripe, and already rotten at the same moment. The ice, the waiter assured us, was special, tourist-class, made from bottled water, although the sight of a small fly trapped in one of the melting cubes failed to inspire my confidence.

After the drinks, I found myself swaying slightly on my way to the restroom. I paused to steady myself on a shelf that housed a collection of curios, bones, and miniature naïf paintings, bright colors still garish beneath a coating of dust. A piranha was preserved whole under a thick layer of varnish, bared teeth still sharp enough to prick my finger. The skin was a dull green, though, nothing like that beautiful string of captured rainbows I had seen on the river.

Next to the piranha there was a mounted skeleton of a larger fish, jaws open to reveal a set of horrifying human molars: the pacu, according to an engraved tag that I had to brush off to read. From the end of the shelf, I picked up an odd piece of something that looked like a rawhide pet treat, yellowed and sharp, slightly twisted at the end.

I was startled by the waiter's voice behind me, too close. He took the piece out of my fingers. "You know this?" he asked, and I shook my head, not trusting my voice to come out steady. "This is the bone of the man part of the boto pink dolphin. You know the story?" I shook my head again.

"The boto likes to party with girls; he likes to drink. If there is a party, then the boto will become a human being and come out of the water to drink and dance with the pretty girls." The waiter waggled his head and shoulders, as if he were dancing to a music that I could not hear. "When he is human, the boto wears fancy clothes, and all the ladies love him. At the party he picks the most beautiful woman and takes her to the river. In the morning he is gone, and then nine months later: baby. If a *caboclo* girl doesn't want to say the father of her baby, she will say it was the boto." He laughed. "If you are at a party and you think maybe this person is really a boto, you just have to take off his hat. The boto always wears a hat because even when he is human he has a breathing hole on the top of his head."

The rest of the dinner is remembered in the dots and dashes of a drunken Morse code. When the fish came, it was a dead thing on my plate, and I could not touch it. We stumbled back to our hotel. My gratitude that the bed was not a hammock filled me with an effervescent happiness as I fell asleep, instantly.

The next day we woke to a sharp rap on our hotel door as the concierge declared in an affronted tone that there was a telephone call for the *senhor*. It was Matt's contact at the university, telling him that his specimen collection trip would leave from the docks in an hour. This type of last-minute surprise, Matt's contact assured him, was completely routine for Brazilians. Matt relayed this to me while he stuffed his dirty clothes back into his suitcase and rifled through mine in search of insect repellant. I squinted at him as the harsh sunlight seeped around the edges of the blinds, too preoccupied with the numbness the liquor had left behind my eyes to worry about finding my way around the city and back to the airport.

That night was the first night of the dreams that would last for the next nine months—so vivid and intense that the reality of the waking day began to recede and seem insubstantial in comparison. On every night, in every dream, I was in the water. Usually I was swimming, powerfully and fast enough to feel the water tugging and smoothing my skin. Sometimes I was swept along by the currents. Occasionally I was pulled under and struggled for the surface. The day that Maya was born, the dreams ended. I still miss that watery world, long for its muted sounds, the weightlessness and endless shades of blue.

I used to wonder, during my pregnancy, if the baby shared my dreams, nutrients and thoughts passing through the umbilical cord to this heartbeat within my heartbeat.

Then, when the dreams stopped so abruptly after her birth, I realized that the opposite was true: The dreams were hers all along; she had shared them with me.

I do not think that Matt noticed the discrepancy in the dates. But I knew that the baby could not be his. There were other signs as well. From the time she was born, her eyes were an odd, dark-gray color that matched neither of our shades of blue. There was the birthmark on the top of her head. And she was always inconsolable if she was away from the water for too long. I had to bring her into the shower or put her in a bath several times a day. By six months she could swim like a fish, although she showed no interest in crawling and never learned to speak. She did laugh, though.

I would take our faculty pass to the university pool and spend hours with her in the water. There, enduring the curious looks from the other mothers, I began to realize that this child was not mine to keep.

Maya was hardly two when she grew sick. Even in the swimming pool, she was quieter. Her skin began to look wrong, a blue shade rising up beneath the pink. I knew, not immediately, but I figured it out.

It makes a certain amount of sense how the child would be human for the first years. This is to recompense the mother for the gestation and birth. After all, those first years are the sweetest: all milky softness and endless caresses. That ought to be reward enough. But, in the end, the boto's child must always return to water.

Leukemia, it turns out, is a very imprecise word. It is a word that doctors use when they really have no idea what is going on. I once thought that if a disease had a name it would have a protocol: a series of steps, procedures, carefully calibrated dosages. And so, if one were careful enough, followed directions precisely, one might be cured. How surprised I was to see the doctors bumbling around like fat, fuzzy honeybees trapped in an overturned jar without the faintest idea of what glass was.

A doctor should be the first to admit how little we understand about the mysteries of life. But it did no good for me to try to explain. When at first I resisted the doctors' recommended course of care, I received a threatening phone call from the Department of Children and Families.

While in the Amazon I'd seen a matamata, a sort of rough draft of a turtle that cannot swim, cannot withdraw its head into its carapace, cannot chew, and has not changed in twenty million years. Closer to home, I think of the monarch caterpillar growing beautiful, delicate wings in the confines of its chrysalis and then fluttering haphazardly all the way to a precise spot in a forest in Mexico. I thought of the virgin birth of Christ. My own situation seemed mundane in comparison. But still, I kept my mouth shut.

As Maya changed and the long waits in doctors' offices and painful and useless tests and treatments forced out our daily visits to the pool, Matt withdrew into his studies and took on new classes and travel responsibilities. Perhaps he sensed that she was not his child. For me, it was simpler not to ask for his help.

When the hospital was quiet and the smell of burnt coffee and microwave soup let me know that the nurses had retreated to their break room, I gently disentangled Maya from the tubes and wires that entrapped her. I wrapped her in my long wool coat and carried her through the hallways. She sat quietly in the front seat of my car. Sometimes her eyes were wide and serious, and sometimes she slept. It was not so far to the beach; the roads were empty as dawn began to wipe the sky clear of gray.

I have always loved the beach in winter, the way the wind blows a person clean, the briny smell tempered by the cold. I carried Maya from the parking lot to the edge of the water, my feet bare and sure in the sand dunes, her arms wrapped around my neck, her cheek on my shoulder. Without pausing, I waded into the water. As soon as the water came up over her legs, I felt her quicken in my arms. When the water came over our waists, her skin began to change, becoming firmer and cool, smooth, the color a light gray now, barely brushed with pink. Here in the Atlantic, my body rocked in the small swells and my feet ached in the cold water, but I remembered in every detail the feel of the boto beneath my hands those years before.

Maya hung in the circle of my arms for only a moment longer before she nosed under, flicked her powerful tail, and swam away, leaving me in the perfect triangle of her wake, which widened around me as I remained still at its center.

Emu

Jessica Zbeida

Lloyd drives his buck knife down until he breaks the breastbone. Then he skewers the breast, bigger than a Thanksgiving turkey, and he and another guy, Jeremiah, I think, hoist it over the fire. A half-dozen other men, some shirtless, all pretty drunk, cheer and raise their drinks. They stand in a semicircle around a red cooler. Men do love their ice chests. Lloyd lifts the cooler's lid and draws out a shiny blue can of beer. He pops it open, takes a long drink, and catches me watching him. He grins and comes over to where I'm sitting with the other women in plastic lawn chairs. He plucks a cigarette from behind his ear.

"Looks good, don't it, babe?" he says and gestures at the roasting carcass.

He expects a compliment, but I'm too angry to play along. He kneels down beside me and leans in for a kiss. I turn away, so he settles for my cheek.

"You stink," I say.

Lloyd shrugs, stands, and lights his cigarette. Without another word, he goes over to stand with the men. Lloyd's my husband, sort of. Four years ago, he came home from work with a plain gold band from J. C. Penney. At the time, I was five months pregnant with Nikki, our daughter. The ring wasn't much, but it bound us together without the bother of a preacher, a church, and a dress that wouldn't fit. My fingers are too fat for it now, so I strung it on a chain like a pendant. Sometimes, when I'm holding Nikki, she grabs the chain, and the ring jangles down to her tiny fingers. Then, memories of life before Lloyd bubble up in my mind, and I get this funny feeling, not so much regret as déjà vu, like I caught sight of a reflection and didn't realize it was my own until I'd stopped to stare.

Dean screams, and all the women look at him and then at me. I go over to my mother. She holds the baby out to me, her face sympathetic. In a year, maybe less, the patience other women feel toward my baby will disappear.

"Poor little Dean!" she says and kisses his bald head. "Grammy loves you."

"He's hungry," I say.

"You want us to keep an eye on Nikki?" she asks.

"Just keep her and that puppy out of the fire," I say. "Thanks."

I carry Dean to the rickety porch Lloyd built behind our tan, saggy trailer. It's warmer than usual for February, but Texas weather changes the moment you get comfortable. The swing creaks as I sit down, but it doesn't break. I unbutton my dress and unzip my maternity bra. Dean quiets down the moment my nipple touches his mouth. He closes his bluish eyes and falls into a trance, opening and closing his hands like a kitten nursing.

About a yard away, a mound of guts and feathers buzzes with iridescent flies. My legs stop pushing the swing. I begged Lloyd to take everything out to the woods. The inedible parts of my pet—its long, black legs with backwards knees, its three-toed feet, its amber-colored eyes and delicate lashes—lie in that pile.

What remains was discarded in the same heap where I dump potato skins, and the sight of it shrinks my chest and makes it hard to breathe. My vision blurs. I need to get up, to find the shovel, to bury what's left. But Dean's still sucking, nearly asleep, and the mother in me won't allow it. He'd wake up.

◈

Four days earlier, a hard wind blew in, bringing warm, gritty air. Dean had a tooth coming in, and I was out of baby Tylenol. He cried nonstop for hours. I tried ice, pacifiers, even my mother's suggestion of a rag dabbed in whiskey, but he didn't stop. Lloyd had the truck, and nobody else would drive ten miles out to our house. Dean cried so much he made Nikki cry, and then I did, too, out of frustration. I picked up the phone to call 9-1-1 but stopped. What would I say? The operator would expect an emergency, and my answer—"My baby won't stop crying"—wasn't good enough.

I had to get out of the house. It was warm, so I took the laundry from the washer, piled it in a plastic hamper, and let my kids cry. As I opened it, the screen door flew back against the trailer. Flecks of paint fell from the siding. The wind took all the world's noise; it was like being in the ocean, where the only sound is the water, and it's so constant that it seems like silence.

When I finished hanging the clothes and turned around, the biggest bird I'd ever seen was staring at me. It looked like an ostrich, but this bird had darker feathers. I thought it might be a mixed breed, like the labradoodle dogs they sell at flea markets.

The bird didn't move—it watched, head cocked to one side. Then it took a breath and ruffled its feathers. I held the plastic hamper in front of me, in case the bird attacked, hoping to intimidate it—they say that works with mountain lions.

"Hey, bird! Go on, now! Get!" I said and raised the hamper.

For good measure, I jumped up and down, but the bird was still a foot taller than me. It seemed more puzzled than afraid, and soon it turned to inspect a pile of leaves. I ran for the front door and locked it, though how the giant bird would've opened it, I can't say.

The kids were still crying. I wrapped an ice cube in a rag and held it to Dean's gums. Eventually, he quieted down. Nikki fell asleep on the couch holding half of a peanut butter and banana sandwich. The moment they were asleep, I got on the phone.

"Van Zandt County Water Supply," my mother said when she answered.

"Mom, it's me," I said. "You won't believe what's in my yard."

◈

I spent most of that day on the phone. Every few minutes, I'd peek out through the dusty curtains. By twilight, Nikki knew something exciting had happened, and soon she was running through the house in her underwear.

"Watch, Momma, watch!" she said and threw herself onto the couch. Then she jumped up, ran back to her room, turned around, and began again. I told her I'd spank her but soon gave up scolding her. Just after six, Lloyd's truck pulled up. He got out and killed the engine but left the headlights on. I opened the door and called to him.

"Lloyd! Come inside!"

“Where is it?” he asked. He pulled a .22 rifle from the truck’s cab. He leaned into the light as he loaded the gun.

“I don’t know.”

“Well, come on,” he said. “Let’s find it.”

“Can’t we leave it alone?”

He didn’t answer. We circled the house, him in front and me behind. Nikki’s voice, softer through the wall, echoed through the rooms. The dark made the trailer a long, black box, a broken train car, but inside, when Nikki laughed, it felt familiar, cozy, like our home.

We got to the front yard without seeing the bird. Lloyd pointed his gun at the ground and pulled a pack of cigarettes from his shirt pocket.

“Will you watch while I take the clothes off the line?” I asked.

He smiled and lit a cigarette. I felt stupid. The bird wasn’t there, and soon Lloyd would start teasing me. Had I been drinking that morning? Maybe the bird also laid golden eggs? His questions were meant to humble me, to show me this was what happened to women who watched too much TV. Lloyd would tell the story at family get-togethers. I undid the clothespins and draped the shirts, pants, and sheets over my left arm.

Lloyd leaned against his truck, blowing smoke rings into the sky. From somewhere out in the falling dark, the bird stepped forward, illuminated in the truck’s headlights. I held the clothes to my chest.

“Lloyd!” I whispered, and pointed.

He saw the bird and raised his gun. I squeezed my eyes shut, waiting for the shot, but it never came. When I opened my eyes, Lloyd was staring at the bird. Flecks of white in its gray-black feathers caught the light like sequins. At least now Lloyd wouldn’t get to ask me stupid questions, or at least not the *same* stupid questions.

"It's an ostrich, right?" I asked.

"Nah, it ain't," he said. "It's an emu."

"A what?"

"Emu. People raise 'em to eat. One guy out in Wills Point has near one hundred head," he said.

"This thing walked forty miles?"

"It's probably from close by," he said. "I'll give Arnie a call. Bet he's heard something."

Lloyd unloaded his gun and switched off the truck's lights. He grabbed a bag of groceries from the floorboard and shut the door with his boot.

"Come on," he said and walked toward the trailer. We went right by the emu, and it didn't move except to turn its head. Lloyd seemed so calm. Had I overreacted? What if I *was* one of those women who watched too much TV?

When we came inside, Nikki latched onto Lloyd's leg. He set the groceries on the counter and picked her up. He lifted her over his head and blew on her bare, pot-bellied stomach until she squealed with laughter. The noise woke Dean, and he started to cry.

"You get the baby Tylenol?" I asked.

"In the bag, honey," Lloyd said.

"Dinner's in the oven," I said and dug through the groceries until I found the Tylenol. After a dropper full, Dean slept for the rest of the night. The quiet felt so eerie I went to check on him twice to make sure he was alive. His face was as smooth as a porcelain doll's.

Lloyd ate dinner on the couch. The Mavericks were playing somebody, maybe the Lakers. I fed Nikki, gave her a bath, and put her to bed. Lloyd fell asleep with the game on, the empty plate balanced on his lap. He didn't move when I took it. He slept through half the game while I did the dishes and packed his lunch for the next day. He snored in a soft, even rhythm. I'm so used to it that I can't get to sleep when he's gone. Lloyd's still handsome. He's twenty-nine, two years younger than me. His nails are greasy, and his hands always smell mechanical. Like his snoring, the smell's so familiar to me that I prefer it to cologne.

With slow, quiet steps, I went to him and kissed his forehead, and Lloyd opened his eyes.

"Mmm," he said. "Kids asleep?"

"Yeah," I said. "What'd Arnie say?"

"Said it's an emu. Guy in town has some. Might be his." Lloyd shifted his weight and put one hand on the back of my knee.

"You coming to bed?" I asked.

His hand slid up my leg, out of practice rather than desire.

"Soon as the game's over," Lloyd said.

I turned off the lights and got into bed. The wind shook the trailer all night. My dreams frightened me awake, and when Dean cried out just before dawn, I was glad to get up.

◈

It was calm the next morning, with clouds stretched in a high, lacy tablecloth from one horizon to the other. I stacked two bags of trash and a bucket of kitchen scraps by the door. The trash can sat next to the front door, but the scraps had to go out behind the house. I took the broom in case the emu attacked.

Leaves crunched under my shoes as I walked around the trailer, holding the slop bucket in one hand and the broom handle in the other. Squirrels barked in the treetops; they chased each other down spidery branches, and the commotion sent acorns tumbling to the ground. Nikki sang along with a girl on *Sesame Street*; I knew the melody from a church song.

The emu wasn't there, and I hurried over to the weedy

patch Lloyd planned to use as a garden. I lifted the bucket, and the scraps hit the ground with a wet thud. Branches cracked, and the emu ran forward, feathers spread like some black angel.

I raised the broom and held my breath, but the emu stopped at the scrap heap. It bent its head to sniff the rubbish, and then it dug in.

"Were you hungry?" I asked. The emu ate everything—it gobbled up potato skins, banana peels, and stale heels of bread. As it ate, it raised its head and swallowed with two jerks of its long neck. I lowered the broom and watched. I'd never been this close to such a large, strange animal, and it thrilled me. The emu bent its knees backwards and sat down. It ate quickly for an animal without hands. Each time it lifted its head to swallow, the sun caught its feathers. They glinted yellow, purple, and turquoise all at once, like gasoline in a puddle.

When the emu finished the scraps, it rooted through the grass for crumbs. There weren't any, so it turned its head to nibble its feathers.

"Why did you come stay with us?" I asked.

The emu's head bobbed as it preened. The skin around its eyes had the silvery glitter of a waitress's eye shadow. All its attention was focused on grooming; I envied such dedication.

"I hope you stay," I said.

The emu turned its round, brown eyes on me and seemed to understand. I wanted to touch it, to find out how its feathers felt, but I was afraid I'd scare it away.

◈

The next day was Thursday. Lloyd likes to fuck on Thursdays. It helps him relax enough to get up for work on Friday. Otherwise, he'd sleep through his alarm clock or call in sick. Some Thursdays I feel like it, some Thursdays I don't, but I always give in when he kisses my neck and then my ear, working his way around to my mouth.

That day, he held out for eight minutes, which was long enough for me to enjoy it. I put on my T-shirt after we finished and laid my head on his chest. He wrapped his arm around me, and his heartbeat thumped in my ear.

"Better?" I asked.

"Much," he said. "What about you?"

"I always feel better," I said.

His chest was pale and almost hairless, so different from his tanned, oil-stained arms.

"I asked Arnie about the emu," Lloyd said.

"What'd he say?"

"He said you dress it like a deer. The meat's real tender, ideal for grilling."

I propped my chin on his chest and looked at him. "So?" I said.

Lloyd shrugged. "Arnie's gonna help me dress it after work tomorrow. I invited your mother and a few other people over on Saturday. You can make that potato salad you like. Get some beer, some charcoal, and we'll be eating for days—"

"You're going to kill it?" I asked. I sat up and pulled away from him.

"Well, yeah," he said. "Why not?"

"But it hasn't done anything," I said.

"Why are you so upset, baby?"

"Because it doesn't make sense, goddammit!" I said.

Lloyd leaned forward and hugged me. He wanted me to lie down beside him and be quiet, but I wouldn't.

"Please don't do it, Lloyd. For me," I said.

"You want to keep it? Like a pet?" he asked. "We don't have room for that, Beth. Where are we gonna get money to build a pen or to feed it?"

"Can't we just leave it alone?"

"It came here. If it leaves, fine. But if it stays, we're gonna eat him," Lloyd said.

I took a blanket and a pillow and went to sleep on the couch. Lloyd was wrong, and he'd have to admit it. I wanted him to apologize, to thank me for all my work, for everything I did for him and our kids. Then I'd forgive him. We could pawn my too-small ring and build an emu pen. Nikki would run around, and Dean would take his first steps, and my life would be better, easier to bear.

None of this happened, though. Soon, Lloyd's snores filled the house.

◈

Dean's tooth bothered him again the next day, and Nikki wanted to watch and re-watch *Sleeping Beauty* every hour and a half. Dean didn't cry, but he wouldn't take his bottle. Nikki spent the morning dancing through the house in one of my old nightgowns, singing along to the movie. By lunch, she'd watched it three times. If I had money to buy any other movie, I'd destroy this one just to escape the songs. Dean finally fell asleep after I got him to nurse, and by then *Sesame Street* was on, so Nikki gave up *Sleeping Beauty*.

"Mommy's going outside," I said. "Come get me if Dean wakes up, okay?"

"Okay," she said. "Look, Big Bird has a teddy bear. Like mine."

"Yes, he does," I said. "Someone must love him."

"I love him," Nikki said.

It was chilly outside in just my housedress and slippers. The emu wasn't around, so I went around the house, calling it. I kept going like that, around and around, screaming for the animal. As soon as I got to the backyard, I thought I heard it in the front, and when I got to the front it wasn't there but in the back.

In my rush, I hit a stump and fell face-first into the leaves. It happened so fast my arms didn't break the fall. I laid there, breathing ragged through my mouth. A musty, brown smell surrounded me. My shin throbbed, and I felt a lump that would become a dark bruise. I spat out a leaf. The pain surprised me when I pulled a chunk of bark out of my leg. Blood beaded up in a red pearl.

I hobbled over to a swing set my mother bought for Nikki. The swings are tiny plastic squares suspended on skinny chains. A warning sticker says it shouldn't be used by anyone weighing more than 100 pounds, which definitely includes me. Still, I squatted down and waited for it to collapse, but it didn't. A red-breasted robin landed on the slide. It hopped twice, chirped, and took off again.

Then the emu appeared. It walked slowly, stretching its head forward like a horse that knows its master has a sugar cube. My leg throbbed, and I closed my eyes for a moment. The emu might bite or attack. It might have a terrible disease.

The emu turned its head to look at me with both eyes. Its legs were strong, brown-black, and scaly. The wind rustled the leaves, and the emu blinked. It circled the swing set and sat down. I reached out my hand, and the emu sniffed my palm. It wanted food. When it didn't find any, the emu took my thumb in its beak. It didn't bite—it was more like it wanted to shake my hand but didn't have the required equipment. The emu's tongue touched my thumb, and then it let me go.

"You have to leave," I said.

The emu searched the leaves for bugs.

"Please," I said. "Lloyd won't let you stay."

The emu found a pecan and raised its head to swallow

it. The bird was calm, happy, but Lloyd would back in a few hours.

"Go on, now," I said and stood up.

I leaned against the swing set and waved my right arm over my head.

"Go on, now! Get!" I yelled.

The emu rose and watched me.

"You have to go!" I said. "Now, get! Get out of here!"

The emu didn't understand, so I hopped forward and pushed it. The bird's body was warm and muscular under its feathers, but it didn't budge. I tried again, and the emu stepped back. My feet slipped on the leaves, and I fell. The emu cocked its head and leaned over me. An endless blue sky surrounded its dark head. I threw a handful of leaves at it.

"Please go!" I said. "Please go away."

The emu turned away as Nikki opened the front door.

"Mommy?" she called. "Dean's crying again."

"Okay, baby," I said and limped back to the house.

"Why are you crying, Mommy?" she said. "Are you hurt?"

I scooted her back inside.

"Yes, baby," I said. "But it's my fault."

◈

I'm not a person who prays, but I got as close to it as I ever have that night. Each time the meat tenderizer hit the pork chops, I whispered *please leave, please leave,* over and over. Once dinner was in the oven, I waited on the front porch for Lloyd. Dusk painted the sky a deep turquoise, and a bone-white half moon rose over the pasture. Far off, the neighbor's dairy cows lowed, each waiting its turn in the stall.

If the emu wasn't around, Lloyd might give up. He'd worked all day, and if I got him in front of the TV and fed him dinner, he'd fall asleep and forget the whole thing. I hoped so, anyway. The sky was blue-black when two sets of headlights came toward the trailer. Lloyd's truck pulled in first, and behind him was Arnie, his mechanic boss and fishing buddy. I like Arnie, but that night I could have strangled him. They left their trucks running.

"Come here, Beth," Lloyd said. "I got something for you."

"I chased it off," I said and walked over.

"Aw, damn!" Arnie said. "I was looking forward to that barbecue! Your potato salad's the best, Beth."

Some other time, I'd play the housewife and thank Arnie.

"I lost the recipe," I said.

Lloyd reached into his truck and pulled out a curly haired, wriggling puppy. He held it out to me, but I didn't take it.

"Got you a pet, babe," he said and smiled. He sat the dog on the ground, and it pranced off toward the brush. A moment later, the puppy growled.

"Listen!" Lloyd said.

The emu stepped out of the dark, its feathers reflecting moonlight.

"There he is," Arnie said.

He reached into his truck for a rifle. Lloyd did the same, and soon both were armed. My stomach dropped and my mouth went dry. The puppy circled the emu, barking.

My leg screamed with pain, but I ran toward the emu, shaking my arms and screaming like someone possessed. The emu didn't run—it watched while Lloyd drug me across the yard.

"Leave it alone!" I yelled.

Lloyd sat me down on the front steps. My breath came too fast. I'd never cried so hard, not when I was in labor or when my cat Biscuit got run over. He looked at me like I was a math problem, something too complicated to understand.

"Beth," he said. "What's going on here? Talk to me."

But I couldn't. When I tried, my words were sobs that didn't make sense.

"Jesus," Arnie said. "If it was a kitten, maybe, but this..."

Lloyd stroked my hair. He spoke in a voice he used to read Nikki stories.

"Take the puppy inside," he said. "You know I'm right."

"Lloyd—" I began.

"It's for the best, Beth," Arnie said.

"It really is," Lloyd said.

Whether I threw myself over the emu or tied myself to it with a rope, in the end they would win—I'd have to give up and go back to my life, to taking care of Lloyd and the kids. Even if I convinced Lloyd not to do it tonight, he could wait until I dropped my guard.

Snot left a shiny snail's trail when I wiped my nose on my sleeve. I limped back to the emu. It stepped over to me, and I held out my hand to it. Its bird breath tickled my palm. The country music station on Arnie's radio filled the yard with the twang of steel guitars.

"I'm so sorry," I whispered.

The emu bent its head to pick at the gravel. I sunk my hand deep into its feathers and felt the warmth of its body.

"Wait until I'm inside," I said, and Lloyd nodded.

I crossed the yard, and the puppy trotted after me. When I got to the trailer, I picked it up. A square of the living room glowed through the screen door. Nikki sat on the couch, swinging her legs and picking her nose. She wouldn't remember the emu in two weeks, maybe less. She leapt off the couch the moment she saw the puppy.

She ran to the door and yanked it open. Behind me, two shots cracked the night open.

The puppy barked at Nikki, and she reached out for it. The puppy nuzzled her face and licked her cheek. She laughed, and I knew she was happy.

"Look, Momma, he likes me!" she said.

She hugged the puppy and closed her eyes. My mind fixed the image of her face, innocent and blissful, to remember on hard days.

With Sheep

Carol Guess & Kelly Magee

1.

Drive, she said, so I did, and then I said, Where to? and she said, I don't know, south? so I veered onto the interstate and gunned it for lord knows where, weaving through traffic like I knew where I was going, her beside me with feet on the dash, knees open, pants soaked. Do you got the book? she said, and I said, I got the book, and then I glanced into the back seat to make sure I had the book, and it was right there like it'd been the whole last month, this kind of thing not known for its predictability, due dates ranging over several weeks, symptoms unclear—she'd been shedding a lot, could that be a sign?—the best advice the doctor could, *would*, give being, You'll know it when it happens. How will we know? we wanted to know, but her doctor was a prick who thought all woolies should be quarantined or banished, and once he got the tests back he asked us to seek help elsewhere, knowing there was no help elsewhere, knowing there was no elsewhere. Once her coat came in, she couldn't even ride the bus without getting dirty looks. Even her parents disowned her, the hypocrites. I told them right to their faces. What's that you're wearing, I said, and is it or is it not made from animals?

Her dad had on a wool sweater. I could tell. He said, Not those kind of animals.

That's what you think, I said.

Her mom said, You two are determined. I can see that. Where will you do it?

Here was where my girl finally chimed in. In a field, she said quietly, like she was in a trance. In the moonlight. Under a spring shower.

She's lost her mind, her dad said.

Had to admit, I thought so, too.

We weren't so much determined as desperate. Her parents could've given us the money we needed, but when she asked, her dad gave her a book about financial planning instead. It was called *The Richest Man in Babylon: The Success Secrets of the Ancients.* The first piece of advice was "start thy purse to fattening." So that was what we did.

Now here we were, driving south to nowhere special, toward the big unknown, and I was terrified that the big unknown would come shooting out of her the wrong way, backward or upside down, maybe drenched in blood, maybe strangled by its own cord, and I'd be the only one on deck, standing there with my thumb on chapter nine. I hadn't studied enough. I sucked at exams. The test material was all half-wrong anyway, designed for vets and pawned off on woolies like they didn't still have human anatomy. The factory people had assured us that she'd go back to being a normal girl within a few weeks of delivery. The injections, they said, are simply for the health of the fetus. The meds may cause some *completely reversible* changes in your girlfriend here, but hey, they said, it'll make her hair nice and thick! Then they'd nudged me and said, Some of the side effects you might enjoy! I still didn't know what they'd meant by that.

Pull over here, now, she said suddenly, so I did because she was panting and grinding her teeth, and because I didn't know where I was going anyway, although she could've picked a friendlier spot, this one being the side of the road and all, and beyond that miles and miles of snow-covered nothing. I grabbed the book and got out, and she twisted free of her clothes and fell onto the gravel, chest heaving. I'd be lying if I said she looked even partly human then. But she wasn't animal either. Three months ago, she'd started covering her body like other woolies, even around me, so it'd been a while since I'd seen her bare skin, but when I rounded the front of the car I could see that she didn't have bare skin anymore—she had this white fur, thick but short, darker in the places she sweated.

I couldn't help it. I bent down and petted her.

The fur looked so soft and my god, it felt even softer, like mink, I thought, though I'd never touched mink, and I confess, yes, my first thought was that if this baby was anything like its mother then we were going to get a lot for the trade. We were going to be set for some time.

She'd been lying on her side, groaning, but she shot up after I petted her, got on all fours and tried to kick me with her hind leg. I yelped. She panted and put her head down. I could see that a single leg was hanging out of her. There was no head. That wasn't good.

I'm dying, she said. Help me.

Remember, I said, it's completely natural. This was what she'd told me to tell her, but she didn't seem to want to hear it now. Her eyes glassed over, her face retreated into itself, and she screamed.

I'm a beast! she said. It hurts!

Just calm down, I said. That wasn't the right thing to say either.

She tried to kick me one more time; then her leg twitched around like a dog with an itch, and she ran away across the snowy field. *Ran* is the wrong word. She was still on all fours. I guess what she did was she galloped.

Where are you going? I shouted. I opened the book in my hands. I looked up *malpresentation of the fetus.* I scanned the words, barely able to make sense of them. *You will need to push the fetus back into the uterus,* I read. *You can use the eye sockets to pull out the head.*

I looked up. She'd stopped galloping and now lay in a heap in the snow.

2.

You looked up. I'd stopped running and now lay in a heap in the snow.

You were waiting for me to birth what would market.

You were waiting for money to fall from my purse.

Here's the secret I'd been keeping under all my fine white fur: no way in hell was I selling my baby. My baby it was, not ours, not yours. My baby's leg, dangling. My baby, struggling to meet me in cold night air. *Woolie*, you called me, like I was a rug. Not human, not animal. Just rolled up to trade.

The car panted on frozen gravel. You stepped toward me, then stopped. Put your head in your book. *Calm down.* Paging through chapters. *You can use the eye sockets to pull out the head.*

It was enough that you wanted to sell my baby, but I'd seen the way you looked at my fur. It was common in humans; all woolies said so. You'd put a price on my baby and a price on me, too.

I inched backward, then took off running. Keys in the car, car in drive, driver driving. With a frozen heart still I knew what to do. South, toward snow and something else. If

I could get there before the birth. If I could get there at all.

From a distance I watched myself drive, fur fumbling the quicksilver wheel. I watched myself swerve, blood on my thighs, and I watched myself suck on my pain like a lozenge. The barn appeared so quickly that I drove past it, then spun a U-turn on the interstate. Over the median, across winter fields until the car said stop and crashed into a tree.

I don't remember leaving the car or stumbling across the field to the barn. But I remember the door, marked just as she'd promised. No key but a password. The password was *lamb.*

When we stopped being the same (that is, while you stayed stuck in your human ways and I fell in love with my animal instincts), we stopped believing the same stories. You took your news straight, headlined and viral. I bent my ear to what bleated or snaked. There's an underground to every location and at least two versions of every escape.

When I woke up I was surrounded by sheep, and my baby was missing. The sheep were circling something. Licking it clean. Black fur wet from blood and tongue. I bent toward her, put my mouth on her, and cleaned my blood from my baby's eyes.

You said I'd change back, that my wool would recede and my skin show taut. You said my humanness would erase all traces of a woolly birth. You said these things because you wanted my baby whether or not I survived the birth. But what had changed in me had made me whole. Now I was who I'd always been. I curled up with my lamb. We slept with our flock.

In the morning, I watched through the diminishing veil of language as my farmer-protector (body like love was once your body) opened the giant door and herded my flock, my family, into a pen.

This was not a slaughter, but a shearing. She'd promised me sanctuary: we could live till we died.

It took a while for her to notice the two of us. I wasn't on my feet just yet, afraid to leave my baby's side.

When she noticed, she smiled. Said something in the language I used to know; it was leaving me, language.

She stroked our wool.

Pelicans

Julian Hoffman

The sun was high, insistent, and brought with it the hazy gauze that garlands these lakes in summer. Last night's stubborn winds had pushed off sometime after sleep, leaving a strandline scribbled with lost wood and wracked weeds. The pelicans had woken me at first light. They were fitfully feeding alongside cormorants in the lagoon. Each morning I'd witnessed the same frenetic ritual of thrashing and churned water, a gossipy chattering and clapping of bills. The pelicans would flare out, then circle in clamoring numbers to trap shoals of small fish in the shallows, where they're scooped into the birds' inflated pouches as easily as handfuls of sand. I'd spent the morning photographing them, taking notes regarding their behavior, numbers, and feeding patterns, occasionally being interrupted by footsteps sloshing at the water's edge.

He was closer now, closer than he'd been all week. I decided to speak to him.

"*Kalimera*."

"*Kalimera*." He turned on the last, drawn-out breath of

the greeting, having offered a momentary glance. His eyes were deep, buried beneath thick lashes like awnings lowered against the light. He neither challenged nor questioned, simply noted my presence as he turned and walked away, receding along the quiet shore.

I suppose I'd watched him as he had watched me. Each day he'd wandered the dog- and otter-paw pocked sands, shuffling weeds and bleached shells with his feet, fumbling in the pockets of his loose trousers for a cigarette to draw on before settling on the shore to strike a hand-sheltered match. At times he would perch like a heron on the upturned hull of an unused fishing boat, a study in poise. He was probably in his late sixties, and he moved sparingly, with gentle precision. Occasionally I saw him sitting cross-legged or crouched on the small rise of dunes pitched away from the beach, with his back to the dense reed bed that swayed and cracked with the slightest provocation of breeze. Mostly though, he stared. He would look out over the limpid waters of the lake as though assigned a watch, tracking the stillness, memorizing the empty spaces as if they contained an invisible design, something necessary.

◈

I'd studied marine sciences at the University of Toronto. After completing my degree I'd read an article about the plight of the Louisiana brown pelican—how the widespread use of DDT in the 1950s and '60s had completely wiped out the coastal population. The toxic chemical didn't affect the pelicans immediately but killed them off slowly and indirectly. It was absorbed into the food chain by small fish as it drained off the agricultural plains of the American heartland and into the Mississippi River. From there it traveled downstream, carried in the tissues of the fish upon which the pelicans fed in the coastal waters. As the chemical accumulated over the years in the pelicans' systems, its effect was to dramatically reduce the thickness and rigidity of their eggshells. Ultimately, the Louisiana brown pelican was extirpated by its nurturing instincts, crushing its own eggs as it sat protectively over them. But with the banning of DDT in 1972, and a concerted restocking program and conservation presence, the brown pelican returned to the shores and barrier islands of Louisiana in healthy numbers.

I was so taken with this heraldic story of the resurrection of a community that I applied for a research post out of Baton Rouge. As part of my work there, I'm sent for a week or so each year to a different pelican colony in another part of the world, an exchange aimed at sharing conservation methods and techniques. It allows me to gain a better understanding of local dynamics and how they potentially affect all preservation schemes.

The Prespa Lakes, where I had spent the last week, sit on the borders of three Balkan countries—Greece, Albania, and the former Yugoslav Republic of Macedonia. The larger of the two lakes resembles the sea in certain lights and is separated from its smaller neighbor by a flat and scrubby strip of land. These lakes are the summer home for more than a thousand pairs of Dalmatian and great white pelicans, and are one of the most important European breeding grounds of the birds. They nest on reedy islands set in open water on the smaller lake, though they tend to feed from the clearer, deeper waters of the larger. Throughout the day the pelicans cross back and forth between the two, appearing as suddenly as apparitions above the road that splits the isthmus.

◈

I looked up from my notes and refocused the telescope on a small group of Dalmatian pelicans idly preening themselves in the shallows. In the still, heat-leavened silence his voice came like a gunshot.

"Where are you from?" He'd approached silently, as I do when studying animals, and had startled me. He'd asked in English, good but accented, which didn't surprise me as I'd met many people in this far corner of Greece who'd emigrated and returned.

"Toronto, originally. But I've been working in the States."

"I don't know much about the States, but I know Toronto pretty well." He stood slightly hunched, as though the best part of his life had been spent in the sitting position. "I've lived for twenty years there. Born here though. You like the pelicans?"

"I'm here to study them."

He watched me carefully, with a hint of a smile. "Fine. But do you like them?"

In the few seconds that hung between question and answer, his eyes, under cover of their generous lashes, had left my own, had betrayed an independence of view and drifted ever so slightly to a space to the right of me and beyond. I turned and looked in the same direction to see seven or eight Dalmatian pelicans gliding toward us, hugging the coast. It was like watching a dream pass, hazy and hypnotic.

"Would you like to look at them through the telescope?" His eyes suddenly left the pelicans, flickered briefly, and refocused. He stood motionless, staring at me through a watery glaze as the pelicans passed beside us, skimming along only inches above the surface of the lake, nicking the water with their wingtips like rows of skipping stones.

"I used to hate them. All of us fishermen around here did. We thought they ate all the fish. Some people here still think so. Used to curse them from the moment we put the boat in."

There was a hesitancy in his speech, a slight tremor born of age.

"There was a time when we got paid for them. Like a pest. We took them to a government office in the nearest town and got fifty drachmas a bird or five for an egg." He laughed suddenly and nodded toward the peaks that climbed away from the lake. "The first time we went, we actually strapped the dead birds to donkeys and walked them over the mountains till we got to the city. You should have seen their faces in the office when we carried these huge dead birds in through the front door. They told us we only needed to bring them the beaks as proof. Now we watch them fly over the same mountains." He was still smiling but shook his head in disbelief—though whether for the past or the present I couldn't tell.

"After this place became a national park, they stopped paying us. We still smashed up the nests, though. We'd scare up all the adults by smacking our oars against the water." *Thwack.* He brought his palm down hard against his thigh. "Then we'd bash the hell out of the eggs and the small ones as they lay there in their nests. Some guys would just hold the baby birds under the water for a few minutes. Said it was easier. When we rowed away, they just floated there limply."

He sat on the sand among my books, and I joined him. I'd encountered these or similar stories before. They were difficult to listen to, but I'd come to accept them as important and necessary, a basic way of understanding why humans persecute certain species. He offered me a cigarette before lighting one for himself. There was a hush over the entire lake basin. Only a drowsy insect hum escaped the filter of mid-afternoon. The last desultory croaks of the marsh frogs had ceased. Dragonflies flitted in their silent and incessant way, as if they were tethered to lengths of taut, invisible string. Water snakes screwed themselves through the sand to bask.

"Do you come back every summer?" I asked him.

He shook his head slowly. "No. It's been many years since I was last here."

"How does it feel to be back?"

"Strange." He reached for a small stone, rubbed it a few times against his fingers, and then threw it into the lake. "But it's always strange to go back. Except for these birds. They're forever coming and going. It's part of their nature. Not ours, though."

"So what brought you back this year?"

Lifting a single eyebrow, he studied me for a few long seconds before finding another stone and casting it into the lake.

A lazy silence ensnared us, but neither of us seemed uncomfortable or bothered. We watched the lake instead. As small groups of pelicans began to gather, to shoulder up together on a narrow spur of sand that reached like a consoling arm around the shallow lagoon, I thought of my time with these birds over the past week. How I'd watched them, mesmerized, as they drifted over the blue lake or climbed in staggered spirals on high thermals. I felt privileged to have shared their pacific space as they set down on the water, barely parting its clear and glassy skin as they slowed to a float. To have woken each morning to see them shoaled before me in a coronation of light.

◆

"It was a day like this, early August." He breached the silence as suddenly as his greeting had. "It had been hot for weeks, and the fish were staying deep. Eleni and I put the boat in from just over there." He pointed to a smooth section of beach to the east of us. "It was one of the old wooden boats. Real heavy and low in the water. We'd proofed it with tar a few days before, so it was even heavier. We were out far when we first felt the wind, really cold. Then the clouds came in from over there."

He drew his arm toward the mountains that towered over the western shore of the lake, the craggy beginning of Albania.

"It was tough getting gas around here so none of us bothered buying motors. I started rowing us back in, but this wind was hard against us, and we were going nowhere. Suddenly it was getting dark, like the sun had gone out, and waves started rocking our boat. The clouds were over the lake now, and there was thunder and lightning everywhere."

He looked up from the sand for the first time since he'd begun talking and turned toward me. "The rain came hard. It was hitting the boat like a hammer. Clouds and fog were all around us, and I couldn't see anything. The waves rose up, way up, out of nowhere. Back and forth they rocked us. Back and forth."

His voice had faltered and trailed off. The lake was like glass today, shimmering beneath a balmy glaze. A kingfisher broke the humid stillness, a tracer of blue light that skimmed the water's edge. We watched it hug the graceful curve of the shore, like the reeds that curled in a sickle of sunlit tassels.

"The water was coming in plenty. We lost our balance in the wind, and she tipped." He said it calmly but with resignation in his voice, like the sound of a slowly deflating balloon. He paused for a few moments, as though re-stitching a loose thread of memory. "We went under. To this day I don't know for how long. A few seconds, a minute. Who knows? I only remember coming up. There was this noise in my ears like a drill, and my chest was on fire. I was scared as hell."

The kingfisher returned along the coast and sped past us like a lit arrow. "You know what, though?" he asked as we gave up trying to follow its flight. "It was the shock of not being above the water—that's what did it for me. All those years of being on the lake, of looking in instead of out."

He looked away again, picked up a handful of sand, and let it fall slowly. The air was thick with silence, stifling and close, and the languid waters lapped out of obligation on the shore. He looked out on the lake as if hypnotized.

"I couldn't see more than a few feet in front of me. The rain was so heavy, and the clouds were on the lake. And then there she was, floating in fog." The sand had run out, but he slowly opened his hand to be sure. He turned abruptly and asked me, "Are you married?"

I stumbled for a moment. "No. I was engaged a few years ago. When I was still at university."

"What happened?"

"I had a choice. To get married or take up a job as a biologist studying pelicans in Louisiana. She didn't want to move so far from her family, so I went south on my own."

"Do you regret it?"

"Sometimes."

"How about today?"

"No." I opened my arms to the lake. "Not in places like this. But we haven't spoken since the day I left. Sometimes I wonder what my life would be like if I'd chosen to stay."

"Sure. But then you would have wondered about the other life. The one if you'd gone." He pointed repeatedly at the sand with a bony finger. "This one."

The man stared at me for a few moments in silence. "We were married in spring, Eleni and me. People came from all the villages around here. For three days and nights it went on. Dancing, eating, drinking. I don't know how many lambs we roasted. We were all poor, but everyone pitched in. It was a hell of a time. Eleni was dancing with her father and looking over his shoulder at me, winking. Then she'd blow me a kiss."

As we sat together on the sand in the burning light, a group of pelicans floated near. Others circled high above us in the impossibly blue sky on a ladder of warm air, or slid so low to the water that they seemed inseparable from it, like a jockey hugging a horse's flanks near the finish line. They passed just above the willow tops on their way to the other lake and their nests, drumming their wings like a deep, measured breath. On other days I had watched them drifting out beyond the swimmers, a few kids screeching and splashing in the lucent waters, whose sun-browned bodies were as smooth as polished stone.

"She was facedown next to the boat when I reached her. I was screaming her name over and over: *Eleni Eleni Eleni.*" He repeated the name like an incantation, whispered as slowly as prayer. "But she just stayed there, like one of those dead baby pelicans."

I drew my knees instinctively toward my chest and held them there, keeping as quiet as I could.

"What could I do?" He slumped further into himself, suddenly appearing as small and frail as an injured bird. "I turned her face toward me, and there was blood all over her forehead. It kept coming and going with the waves." He shook his head as slowly as a pendulum. "She must have come up under the boat after it flipped and smacked her head on the edge. She was unconscious but still breathing. I tried to keep her mouth out of the water by pushing her up against the hull. There was no way I could turn the boat."

Mid-afternoon and a fierce light enclosed us. It was like swimming in a bubble. From the corner of my eye I could make out a hazy group of white pelicans rising through the air like little steps of clouds. To see them like that, at the edge of vision, was like watching them through a telescope when the sun draws vapors off the lake that ripple through the lens. The pelicans, and the world around them, flickered and folded in shimmering waves as though a mirage, distorted and unlikely, but as achingly persuasive as a slowly dissolving dream.

"The rain was awful. I couldn't see through it. I just held Eleni against the boat and wiped the blood from her face. And prayed. At some point I started swimming with her under my arm. Just headed out into the clouds and rain. Then I stopped, and thought, maybe it's the wrong way, and I turned back."

He lifted his eyes from the sand, where he'd been absently drawing circles with his finger, and stared at me with an intensity equal to the slow burn of the afternoon. "I was blind on my own lake," he continued slowly, "a lake I'd known since a boy. I was frightened and confused. Couldn't think straight after finding Eleni. And everything I knew about this place had vanished." Anger had appeared in his voice, but it was tempered by helplessness.

"You see that shore? It's where we tied up our boat each day. And the little white church of St. John, on the hill over there. And that's Golem Grad, that big island in the Yugoslavian part of the lake. At least it was called Yugoslavia back then." He pointed out each landmark, pale against the vast light, by stabbing at the air around him. "They'd all disappeared in the clouds and rain. There was nothing. I knew in my memory where each of them were, but without somewhere to start I was like a stranger. In my panic I was lost. Didn't know a thing about this place."

He rose slowly and stood before me, but he seemed distant now, pale and tired, worn down by the heat. The way summer can drown a day in silence. He turned away as though addressing the lake itself.

"Then I heard something in the storm. Something else. It was faint." He edged a few tentative steps toward the lake. "Somewhere out there." I watched him lean forward, as if in a wind, listening. "It sounded like the church bell in our village. They'll ring it for us when we're pulled from the lake, I thought. A single chime, over and over and over. The bell of the dead."

He exhaled deeply, surrendering to the memory. "I imagined our families and neighbors gathering outside our house, our coffin lids at either side of the door. I'm dressed in my only suit, and Eleni is wearing the pale green dress that we bought for our trip to Salonica. She's got wildflowers on her head to hide the cut, and our little boy and girl are holding hands, staring at us, crying."

He was silent now, lost in the listening. The kingfisher blurred before him, but he remained as still as the reeds in the breathless afternoon.

"The bell was getting louder, closer. And then there they were." He suddenly spun in the sand and faced me excitedly. "Pelicans!" Color had found its way to his face again, which lit up with a grin. "That's what it was. Pelicans. Seven or eight of them passed by like ghosts through the rain and mist. They were so close I could hear their wings, over and over, like a bell. I could feel them even. They were really struggling in the storm, and then they were gone. Just like a dream. I put my arm around Eleni's shoulder and started kicking my legs. I followed the pelicans as best I could, just stared at the spot where I thought they'd disappeared and kept going, following them home."

He smiled as he said the word *home*, as if it were the elusive answer to a riddle. He lit a cigarette and brushed the sand from his trousers, and, with a pointing nod of his head, we began walking along the shore.

"They're better at finding their way in the world than we are. I knew they would pass over our beach. They were trying to get back to the small lake and their nests with the little ones. We finally landed not far from where we started. My brother was there, waiting. He knew we'd gone out in the boat, and he came down in the middle of the storm, praying we'd make it in. He rushed us up to the village and carried Eleni into the house. She was in bed for a week, but she made it."

We walked the last stretch of the beach in silence, lost in our own quiet worlds. We found his pickup truck in the shade of a large willow. He leaned against the door and spoke with lowered eyes fastened on some unmappable place.

"I buried my Eleni this last winter, a long way from here. In a cemetery just outside of Toronto. We always said that we should come back here one more time, to pay our respects. So here I am. We wouldn't have had our life together if it weren't for those birds."

He opened the door to his truck, slid in over the dusty seat, and started the engine. Through the open window he looked up at me and said, "You know what I think sometimes? What if they'd flown over just a little to the left or right of us?"

He was laughing to himself as he pulled the truck off the beach and disappeared up the track, dust and sand clouding behind him.

◈

Evening settled slowly, like pond water disturbed by a fallen branch. I realized long after he'd driven off that I hadn't even learned his name. I started a small fire with driftwood and willow limbs, and leaned back against the dunes. I glimpsed pelicans and cormorants heading home, saw the stars come blinking into night as the sky folded in on itself, and watched the last snatches of gathered light vanish like ghosts over the summer-quiet lake. As I covered the few remaining embers of the fire with sand, I heard a bell somewhere in the distance.

The Weight of Things Unsaid

Sara Dupree

The turtle was the size of a quarter and nearly weightless in my hand. Its miniature claws raked my palm in a pantomime of swimming. It carried the smell of damp soil into my in-laws' warm kitchen.

"Do you want that one to be yours, Mom?" Katie asked.

I nodded and closed my fingers softly to keep the turtle from swimming out of my hand.

"What are you going to name him?" She plucks my sweater sleeve and snatches her hand back.

The turtle's head, smaller than my pinky, poked out from between my fingers. Its tiny black eyes blinked at the fluorescent light. He belonged curled in the dark comfort of his egg, not in this bright kitchen.

"Benjamin," I said without thinking, and then wished I could take it back.

Daniel looked up at me from the kitchen floor, where he

sat hunched over an orange shoebox. His eyebrows scrunched together when he heard me say the name. I'd picked the scab of our shared wound. Benjamin was our Boy Name for the baby my body refused to carry. *We'll call him Benny.* We'd laughed as we listed potential names for our potential baby on a napkin and stuffed ourselves at a pizza buffet. Benjamin felt real to me at that moment. I could picture his pink body curled and suspended inside me. But that was almost six months ago.

My insensitivity toward Daniel washed me with guilt. *What kind of mother*, I imagined him wondering, *gives our never-to-be-born son's name to a turtle?*

I walked over and put my empty hand on his shoulder. His sweatshirt was chilly from the damp fall air, but he smelled warm from the work of digging up the turtle eggs. Caged in my hand, the turtle paddled harder, struggling to escape.

In the box below us, the turtle's five siblings scritched across the smooth cardboard. The sound made me shiver. It reminded me that ice was already forming along the river's edge where we would free the turtles after Katie's educational "encounter with nature" had ended.

"Who wants tea?" Susan, my mother-in-law, called as she filled the teapot, knowing with a mother's intuition that I'd hurt her son.

"No, thanks," Daniel said.

She opened the fridge and stepped away from the door, as if hopeful that its contents would trigger a need she would be able to meet.

"Can I have hot chocolate?" Katie asked.

Susan rummaged through the cabinets, humming a John Denver song.

Daniel shrugged to tell me I'd pressed too much weight on him. Hurt, I crossed the kitchen and scooted a chair close to Katie.

"Take your hands out of those sleeve-cages," I told her, but she was fixated on Susan, anticipating the hot chocolate. Katie had recently been diagnosed with Sensory Integration Dysfunction. Her brain processed information from her senses differently from "normal people," her psychologist explained. Her skin was extremely sensitive, and she kept her hands hidden inside her sleeves to avoid the discomfort of touch. Her occupational therapist told me the muscles in her hands would atrophy if she didn't start using them soon. When I drop her off at kindergarten, she grimaces at the sensation of my arms on her shoulders when I hug her good-bye.

"Do you want marshmallows?" Susan called, still digging through her cupboard.

Katie nodded vigorously. Food, sweets particularly, seemed more important than affection.

"You have to actually *drink* it," I told her. "Not eat it from the spoon like soup."

"I know." Her attention remained fixed on Susan, like a dog waiting for someone to throw a ball.

I glanced out the window where my father-in-law, on his four-wheeler, was returning the shovels to the shed. A few yards away was the pile of dirt where we'd dug up the turtle eggs. We'd marked the spot with a stick tied with neon orange tape when the mother turtle laid her eggs in July. With Katie's help, we'd counted the days on the calendar and marked the week the eggs would hatch. Today was two weeks past the week we'd marked. We thought raccoons had eaten the eggs, but Daniel and my father-in-law decided to dig them up just in case. Six inches under the cold soil they found the batch of baby turtles escaping their eggs with tiny, slow movements.

The neat pile of dirt reminded me of a grave, and of my OB's promise to call when the "tissue" returned from the lab. He'd tried to discuss "options" with me that day at the hospital. Cremation, perhaps? I remember feeling angry when he'd mentioned burial as an option. I was angry at his implication: that the object my body refused to carry was somehow equal in emotional weight to a life—someone who had been here and been seen, touched, and loved. But I was too lost in the haze of medication and guilt to answer.

It had been nearly three months since the D&C. I hadn't received a call from the doctor. I'd skipped my follow-up appointment without even calling to cancel. Maybe Daniel had made arrangements. It would be like him to think I needed shielding from the details. I looked down at the turtle in my hand, trying not to wonder about tissue or location or wasted potential.

And the mother turtle—where was she now? After fattening on minnow and tadpoles in the late summer and early fall, she probably sank downstream and quilted herself in mud at the bottom of the river. Did she wonder where her children were?

It shocks and angers me, those instances when nature is counterintuitive or illogical. A therapist once told me I have "an especially strong sense of *should*." It's just plain wrong that a mother turtle goes through the heat and hardship of laying eggs in the hottest summer, only to have them hatch when the weather turns cold. You *should* lay the eggs in the mud of May, mother turtle, when the soil gives way to your claws much easier than the baked clay of July and your children have a long warm summer ahead after hatching. Mothers *should* nurture, no matter what.

And what about the father turtle? If fish can feel paternal, couldn't reptiles? I fell in love with Daniel the day he told me he kept a tank of convict cichlids in his dorm. He was taking ichthyology and wanted to watch firsthand the male fish carrying their babies around in the safety of their mouths. This is a man destined to be a father, I thought. Even though I didn't want any more children after Katie, I wanted her to have a good father. He'd cried when the ultrasound technician admitted she couldn't find a heartbeat.

Everyone seemed to think of the miscarriage as a death. The OB handed me a stuffed lamb with a halo and wings. Sewn-shut eyes with appliquéd lashes. He recommended a D&C to "get the process over," then left Daniel and me alone in the tiny exam room. Of course he meant the miscarriage. The process I wanted over—this hazy bubble of not-quite-grief—can't be fixed by surgery.

In pre-op, Daniel squeezed my hand hard when the nurse started the IV. He looked confused when she asked me if I remembered her. Later he jokingly called her the "Angel of Death."

"I was your parents' next-door neighbor when you moved back to town," the nurse said. "I was there that day in March. I called the police."

I looked down at the stuffed lamb in my hand and marveled at the serendipity of our small town, where it was this woman's lot to bear witness to my worst moments. Five years earlier, I was a newly divorced single mother living in my parents' basement. Relieved by an early March thaw, I was walking along the river with baby Katie and my two border collies. The younger dog, in a moment of pure exuberance, jumped into a hole in the ice for a swim. I locked eyes with him a moment before the current sucked him under the ice and away.

The nurse heard me screaming and called the police. I wanted rescue divers in wetsuits, but all I got was a young female officer who studied my footprints on the thin river ice and wrote in a notebook.

"Do you have somebody who can stay with you?" she asked me.

I looked away from the hole in the ice and tried to answer but was met with my own distorted face mirrored in her sunglasses.

"She just moved back, and her parents are out of town," the nurse answered for me.

Someone called a matronly pastor from the church I'd belonged to when I was a kid. I watched out the window as the pastor and the police officer spoke to each other in the driveway, heads bobbing sympathetically. The pastor came in without knocking. She made me weak Lutheran coffee and told me to nurse Katie, who was fussing at my feet. "It will make you both feel better."

Later, when Katie was sleeping on my lap, the pastor assured me dogs have their own heaven, separate from humans.

Separate, I thought. What kind of cruel joke is that?

"I'm leaning toward Buddhism," I told her.

◈

From the safety of my in-laws' kitchen I allowed myself a moment of self-pity. Next to me, Katie slurped hot chocolate and marshmallows from a soupspoon. A brown puddle ringed her mug and soaked her sleeve-covered hands. Like the nurse, she'd been present on both my worst days, and I worried how the events may have scarred her. I'd read stress hormones were passed through mother's milk. I patted her arm, but she pulled away from my touch. At that moment, I craved the feel of my missing dog's soft coat. I remembered the times I'd let him sleep on the bed, how he'd lay his head on the pillow and snore like an old man through his black nose. How simple, loving an animal.

Across the kitchen Daniel cupped a turtle in each hand and looked down at the others remaining in the box. He said something too quiet for me to understand.

I walked over and looked with him. The turtles inside had drawn into their shells. Daniel opened his hands to show me two turtles reaching and kicking across his palms. "It's body heat," he said. "If you set them down, eventually they crawl up inside their shells and go to sleep. Watch." He set the one in his left hand in the box. Its motions slowed, then stopped. Head and legs retreated, leaving only shell, a tiny box of potential.

Daniel wrapped his arm around my waist and pulled me close. I leaned into him, weighted by things unsaid. What I still hadn't told him was after the D&C I woke in the recovery room dreaming I was trapped under the ice and sobbing for my lost dog. The nurse asked if I was in pain.

"Yes," I lied. While Daniel was signing my release papers in the clinic office, I begged the nurse for a prescription of something strong to help the pain.

"Tylenol and time." She patted my hand.

What I still hadn't told him was the day my dog was swept away I left Katie on the riverbank. I set her by the skinny trees and crawled across the ice on all fours to the hole where Cody had disappeared. Reaching down into the river up to my shoulder, I felt the rush of current. It would have been nothing at that moment to slide the rest of the way in. When I glanced back at the bank, the nurse was holding Katie in one arm and dialing the phone. They looked smaller and farther away than they really were.

What I still hadn't told him was there are moments when the death of my dog feels sadder to me than the loss of our potential child.

◈

We watched the turtles in our hands, still struggling to swim. After a while, Daniel set his in the box with the others. My father-in-law opened the front door and stepped inside.

Cold fall air drifted into the kitchen. "If you're bringing them turtles to the river, you better do it," he said. "It's getting dark."

Daniel nodded and picked up the box. "Come on, kiddo," he called to Katie. "Time to let these guys go."

My palm was raw from the strokes of the turtle's tiny claws, and I knew it would be a relief to set him free. I also knew it was unlikely he'd survive the winter under the ice—he'd starve or freeze or get eaten. All he was at this moment was the potential of life. But as long as I held him in my hand and felt him scratching against my palm, he was real.

I followed Daniel and Katie out into the cold air and down the steep bank to the edge of the river.

Blue Murder

Suzanne Kamata

On the first day of spring, Keita Hosokawa fell in love with a bird. If anyone had told him a week before that this would happen, he wouldn't have believed it. He was fed up with birds. Specifically crows.

That year, the crows seemed greater in number than ever before. Fatter, too. They feasted at the roadside shrines where humpbacked ladies set out oranges and bowls of cooked rice for their dearly departed. They swooped down on cemeteries and ate the offerings from gravestones. They ate until they were as big as roosters, until it seemed as if the telephone wires would not support them.

As if there wasn't enough food available elsewhere, they fed in Keita's orchard. He could see them from the window as he ate his breakfast—a murder of crows settling in the branches of his pear trees. The sight of them made him weary before the day's work had even begun. He turned away from the window and tried to smile at his son.

Ichiro sat in his high chair, banging his spoon on the

tray. His bib was soaked with drool. "*Wan wan wan!*" he said, barking like a dog.

Keita sighed. He tried to get the boy to say "*otosan*" or even "papa," which was easier to pronounce than the Japanese word for father, but he wouldn't learn. He could say "mama" and make a variety of animal sounds, but he seemed to willfully ignore Keita.

"Papa," Keita said softly, trying once again.

Ichiro's spoon flew out of his spit-slimed hand and onto the floor. "Meow," he said, spotting Kitty in the corner.

"Papa," Keita repeated.

From the kitchen, his wife, Misa, giggled. "Don't feel so bad," she said. "He doesn't see you enough to know who you are. He'll figure it out soon enough."

"He doesn't see me because I'm out in the field trying to protect his legacy," Keita said, feeling suddenly angry. He knew that Ichiro wasn't to blame. He was a baby. He slept almost all the time. When he was a little bigger, Keita would take him out into the orchard and prop him against a tree. "This is all yours," he would tell him, as his own father had once taught him. "Someday you'll take care of these trees."

Even if Keita and Misa had other children, Ichiro, as the firstborn son, was entitled to the family property. The land, with all of its trees and the house, would be passed on just as it had been for generations before.

Normally, Keita's parents were at the breakfast table with them, but they had departed the previous day for Texas to visit Keita's sister. She was a doctor, and she had gone to the United States to do research and learn the latest treatments for kidney diseases. Keita's parents worried about her because she was past thirty and as yet unmarried. It didn't matter to them that she had bought her own house and drove an imported car, or that she could afford annual vacations to Europe. They had hopes of a traditional life for her—one with a husband

and kids. Still, she was allowed to do as she pleased. Keita, as the oldest son, was the one who was bound to follow their desires.

When Keita had turned twenty-nine, his mother had declared that it was time for him to take a bride. He felt the weight of duty and meekly agreed. His first choice of wife, a giggly young woman with waist-length hair and dimples, had seemed to like him but refused the role of farm wife. The next ten women he met had virtually identical reactions. They wanted to have careers in tall, air-conditioned buildings. They didn't want to share the roof with his parents. He was thinking that he might have to settle for a foreign bride, one of the Southeast Asians sent to Japan to marry the country's undesirable bachelors, and he wondered how he would be able to communicate with such a woman. He had never studied Thai or Tagalog, and his English wasn't very good.

But then his luck had changed. A family friend introduced him to Misa, a woman who had grown up on a farm. She knew all about pears—how to pollinate them, how to batten the low branches when a typhoon was approaching, how to turn them into a sweet liqueur. Her hair was short, and she didn't mind getting dirt under her fingernails.

The mayor attended the wedding and made a speech praising their complementary qualities. Keita had always been a dreamy boy, he said, but Misa was of simple tastes and practical, and she would keep him tethered to the earth. They honeymooned in Hawaii, where Keita marveled at the acres of pineapples and sugarcane. What it must be like to be in charge of all that! His family's farm was modest in comparison.

For the first year of their marriage, Keita and Misa had worked side by side among the trees, but then she became pregnant, and nausea and headaches had forced her to stay in the house.

On this day, Keita would be going into the field alone.

Misa would play with Ichiro. Maybe she'd watch the afternoon dramas while he napped. With Keita's mother in Texas, Misa would be able to relax for a change. Keita, too. The bickering women made him feel tired, made him almost want to stay in the orchard.

He scraped the last grain of rice from his bowl and pushed the breakfast dishes away. "I guess I'd better get out there before the crows eat all of my fruit."

Misa murmured her agreement and then gathered up the dishes for washing.

Ichiro said, "Moo!"

◈

He could hear the crows as he stomped onto the field in his work boots. "*Kah! Kah!*" They seemed to be mocking him, telling jokes at his expense.

Keita didn't know how to make them go away. He'd staked a scarecrow—a straw man in a floppy hat, plaid shirt, and worn-out jeans—at the center of the field, but the birds didn't seem to mind. They perched on the dummy's shoulder. He'd then tied aluminum pie pans to the branches of trees, having heard that the metallic brilliance would ward off feathered intruders, but after a day or two of being wary, the crows had returned in full force.

If he'd had a gun, he would have blasted into the trees, but he had no such weapon. A sudden burst of fury sparked him with energy. He filled his lungs and screamed, "Iiiiiiyyaaaa!" He ran through the orchard waving his arms like a madman. The crows lifted into the air, flecking the sky with black. They circled cautiously, and then one brave bird descended toward the trees again.

Keita sighed. If it wasn't crows, it was typhoons. If it

wasn't weather, it was blight. He wished that he could take one season off from farming. A few months in, say, an office would refresh him.

He had been to the doctor recently to find out why he was always so tired. His body felt worn and damaged even though he was just thirty years old. His eyesight was failing, his girth expanding, his intestinal tract rebelling after every meal.

"Too much stress," the doctor told him. "You'll have to stop smoking and drinking, and you'd better find another job."

Keita had laughed. If only it were that simple. He had signed up for a karate class—he'd reached black belt while in college—hoping for physical release. But the weekly sparring matches left him breathless and sore, and he found himself being defeated by sixteen-year-old beginners.

Now, standing in the field, he thought about all the work that had to be done. He knew that he could call on the neighboring farmers to help, since his parents were out of the country, but asking them seemed like too much trouble. All he wanted to do was lie down under the trees and sleep.

Instead, he scrabbled for a stone and tossed it up at a plump black bird. "*Kah!*" The crow ruffled its feathers and fixed its beady eyes upon him, but it didn't fly away. Keita turned from the orchard, from his day's work, and walked down to the river that ran along his property.

He found a broad, smooth stone, and he sat there to contemplate the water. The river gurgled and flowed, and its melody soothed him, a balm for frayed nerves. He listened and watched and succumbed to the caresses of the spring breeze on his face. It was in such a beatific state that he first saw the bird.

She rose a few meters in front of him on blue-tinged wings. He admired the long beak, the crimson breast as bright as a wedding kimono. Her grace, the curve of her neck, made his heartbeat quicken. He had seen spindly legged egrets and mallards in this stream but never such a bird as this. In the deepest part of himself, he began to believe that this bird had been sent to him in this moment of difficulty to ease his pain. It was a wild idea, but he clung to it nevertheless.

He remained as still as the stone he sat upon, not wanting to spook this mysterious visitor. He watched as she dove into the water to catch a fish. The *ayu* wriggled in her beak, but she flew into a nearby tree and stunned the fish with a quick slap against the bark before gulping it down.

What kind of bird was she? And where had she come from? He would ask his friend Junji. Junji was a serious birdwatcher from way back. He had a life list of all the birds he wanted to see. Junji's vacations were always part of his quest to check off the birds on the list. He'd ventured as far away as Brazil to catch sight of a parrot in the wild. On a trip to the state of Washington he'd been lucky enough to see a bald eagle. His mind was an encyclopedia of bird lore.

Keita stayed by the river all morning watching the bird. He went back to the house for lunch, but he didn't tell Misa what he'd seen.

"How did your work go?" she asked him, dishing out curry over rice.

"Fine," he said. He could not meet her eyes. He imagined Misa crying out in jealousy. "What?" she might say. "You prefer her company to mine? What about your family? Ichiro? Me?" But in reality, if he told her the truth she would probably chastise him for wasting the morning, not for being unfaithful.

He returned to the riverside after lunch, but the bird was no longer there. After an hour's vigil, he went back to his pear trees. That night he called Junji.

"Sounds like a kingfisher," Junji said. "But that's impossible. They don't live around here."

"Maybe it got lost," Keita said. "Or it might have escaped from a zoo."

"Or maybe you need new glasses."

Keita didn't laugh. Tomorrow morning he would bring his camera. He would show Junji that he wasn't dreaming.

◈

The next day she was there, swooping through the trees on cobalt wings. He wondered if she had a nest nearby. He imagined eggs and then a flock of kingfishers to fly through his mornings.

He hid in the bushes, and when the bird settled for a moment on a black pine branch, he clicked the shutter. He used an entire roll of film. At dusk he returned to the house, reluctantly.

"You're late," Misa said over her shoulder. She was in the living room, seated on the straw-mat floor with the baby.

"I know. Sorry." Keita saw his dinner laid out on the table and knew that it was already cold. He sat down to eat.

In the early days of their marriage, Misa would have sat down beside him while he dined, even if she had already eaten. But now the baby took up almost all of her time. Keita could hear her singing to him now: "Flying crows, why do you call? 'Cause on the mountainside we've seven, seven little babies with lovely round eyes."

She had the voice of a lark, but he hated that song. The crows that plagued his orchard were not pretty. They were like creatures from a nightmare. He'd heard of two schoolchildren being pecked by them. They dropped pebbles on the railroad tracks, messing up train schedules. So what if, according to legend, crows pulled the sun into the sky each day? The birds were a nuisance at best, and there was nothing lovely about their eyes.

He wanted to tell Misa to stop singing, but Ichiro began clapping his hands in delight.

The two of them were perfectly content without him. He felt that he was nothing more than a field hand or a houseboy.

◈

When Keita developed the film a few days later, he was disappointed to find that none of the pictures had turned out. In some, the bird in flight appeared as a blur across the center of the photo. Others were underexposed or awash with light. Nevertheless, he showed them to Junji.

"Could be a kingfisher," Keita's friend mused, squinting at the glossy prints. "But they're usually more skittish around humans."

"I was well hidden," Keita said. Or maybe he had a special affinity with the bird. Maybe she trusted him more than she did other people. This thought warmed him.

He considered telling Misa about the bird, waving the photos in front of Ichiro's face, but they had so much else to interest them—their songs, their kisses, their secret games. No, he would keep the bird for himself.

"Have you outwitted the crows?" Misa asked the next morning.

Keita sighed. He'd covered the trees with netting, but a few of the black demons had found an opening. Those that couldn't get in had spent the morning tormenting the cat.

"Crows are omnivorous," Junji had told him. "They'll eat anything."

Even Kitty, who slept at the foot of his futon? Well, maybe. He'd read an article in the newspaper about crows attacking baby squirrels in another town. The birds nudged the squirrels off the telephone wires and then ate them after they'd fallen to the ground. The reporter had called the birds "a new type of serial killer."

"Please don't speak to me about crows," Keita told his wife. He knew that she didn't really care about what went on in the orchard. She was just making conversation. He wished they had more to talk about, like in the old days before their marriage when they had been a mystery to each other.

Keita knew that there was work to be done, but on this morning he didn't even pretend. He loaded his video camera with a fresh tape and marched straight to the riverbank. Why hadn't he thought of this earlier? With a video he would be able to capture the grace of the bird as well as her delicate shape and brilliant colors.

Keita crouched in his usual spot behind a bush. The grasses there had become matted down from his daily vigils. He held his camera at the ready for an hour and then two, but the bird—his bird—never showed. *The crows,* he thought, his stomach sickening. *The crows have murdered my lovely bird.* If they were brave enough to dive at humans and hungry enough to eat squirrels, then wouldn't they attack smaller birds as well? He tried to muster hope, but after five hours, he left the riverbank and returned to the house.

As usual, dinner was on the table, but Keita ignored the grilled fish and soup. He poured himself a cup of chilled sake and took a big gulp.

"What is it?" Misa asked, the baby on her lap. She had a rattle in one hand, and she reminded Keita of a court jester. There was no way she would ever be able to understand his sorrow.

In his dreams that night, the kingfisher glided on air, circling ever closer to Keita's hiding place. He sat transfixed. The bird, no bigger than a swallow, landed on his palm. She studied him with curious brown eyes and let him stroke her blue back with one finger. And then she ruffled her feathers and flew off into the sky.

Keita woke with a kernel of hope nestled in his heart. Today she would be there, waiting in the trees. He was sure of it as he bolted out the door without eating any breakfast. More than food, more than air, he needed a glimpse of his beautiful bird.

The sun rose higher in the sky as he stared at the river. The fish swam, undisturbed. Sparrows fluttered past, but there was no flash of blue. No long-beaked lover roosting on his palm. And then he heard a crack of twigs and saw the grasses twitch and part, and there was Kitty, with a gift in her mouth. Keita stared in horror, not wanting to believe he had shared his bed with this animal.

The bird's once resplendent plumage was now matted and mauled. Its entrails leaked out through a ripped seam in its chest. One leg was bent, the claw dangling. Its bright eyes were now opaque, unseeing. A bright blue feather stuck to Kitty's fur like a macabre corsage.

Keita's eyes filled with tears. He took off his glasses, and the bird deposited at his feet by Kitty became as blurry as it had appeared in the failed photos. The cat rubbed against his legs, and he kicked her away. For so long there had been nothing bright in his life, and then when this wonder appeared, he had found joy. Yet he couldn't protect this wild thing from danger. And he couldn't protect his orchard—the trees that he had been entrusted with, that he was meant to maintain for Ichiro and all the generations to follow.

His hands trembled as he reached down and scooped up the dead kingfisher. The body was still warm, but there was no heart beating against his palm. With one thumb, he stroked the feathers, and then he laid the bird back down on the ground and began to dig with his bare hands. The dirt flew into the air. It fell on his head, but he didn't care. When he'd dug a deep enough hole, he settled the carcass at the bottom and filled it back up. He found some large stones by the river and laid them on top of the grave. Then he crouched there, behind the bushes, and tried to rock the sudden loneliness out of his body. His grief was so absorbing that he didn't hear the bird calls at first.

"*Kah! Kah!*"

He looked over his shoulder and saw a black-headed figure flapping its wings. It was even larger than the jungle crows that harassed his orchard. The thing came closer and closer, but he wasn't afraid. Beside it, a taller creature picked through the grasses on elegant long legs, its pure white plumage dazzling in the sunlight.

He imagined being lifted by those great white wings, being carried away from the river, skimming over the tops of the pear trees in his orchard, and then continuing across the Pearl Bridge and beyond. He would leave all of this behind and travel to another country. Maybe he would work in an office, or in a clean, bright store. Maybe once he was gone, his wife and son would finally appreciate him. Perhaps they would think he had joined the ancestors and pray to his photo, setting out his favorite foods every morning at the altar. Meanwhile, in some other land, he would find respect and love. There would be no more crows, no more Kitty. He would begin again.

"We brought you breakfast," a voice called out.

Keita stood up and shook away his fantasy. He brushed the dirt off his pants.

"You didn't eat," the voice sang. "You must be famished."

His stomach rumbled as if in reply. He rubbed the tears from his eyes and put his glasses back on. Yes, he was hungry. Taking a deep breath, he flew to meet them, his wife and his child.

Bad Berry Season

Melodie Edwards

On Thursday we got a call from the garbage man that something had been raiding the dump on the edge of town. We told him that if he had a problem with dogs to call the sheriff. But he said, no, this was no dog. This was something big. It had torn a hole the size of a picture window through a garage door and had overturned two Dumpsters as if they were made of Styrofoam. And that wasn't half of the damage. He wanted to know who was going to be paying for all this.

We came out and looked around. Or I did, I better say. Working for the government, I guess I use the collective pronoun a lot without even thinking about it. I/We recommended a thorough cleanup. I explained that a good, strong smell could carry on a medium-sized breeze for miles, even the ten miles up the river across the valley to the mountains where bears usually chose to keep their anonymity. But this wasn't a normal bear year, I explained. This was a drought year, a bad berry season, which meant that starving bears, preparing for a long winter's nap and in dire need of body fat, came in search of dependable meals. Human garbage would do just fine.

"We've already had to put down two of them this year," I told him. "Vandalizing people's cabins for their hummingbird feeders. One of them came in through the roof."

But Mr. Garbage Man just stood there in his bib overalls and looked at me sideways. His name was Marlowe Russell. He'd graduated two years ahead of me from Point-of-the-Rocks High School and now had two kids, each with their own 4-H lamb. And there I was in my uniform, telling him.

"He'll be back tonight," I told him. "Unless you do something about the smell of garbage. Could you move all these Dumpsters inside the shop or somewhere?"

"Nope," he said, and after that I left.

◈

Four days later, the bear made a rare daylight appearance at the Dumpster out behind the taxidermy place, half a block downwind from the garbage heaps. Jep, my ex-boyfriend and the taxidermist in town, called and, pretending not to recognize my voice, asked for my supervisor. It was noon. We were on our lunch breaks, talking over strategies for handling a new roadless area that had just been closed down to four-wheelers where we were having a lot of non-compliance. It was that kind of hunting season. The early snows had brought the elk herds down to their winter grazing grounds before usual, and it was starting to look as if it might turn into a free-for-all, hunters firing into herds from their vehicles and leaving the wounded to get tangled up in barbed wire fences, only to be found the next spring, their antlers chawed down to nubs by rodents, their carcasses frozen in the contorted shapes of starvation. I wolfed down the rest of my sandwich while my boss, Mack, got the details. Then we loaded up the truck with anything we could think of to deter bears. We were on the scene in twelve minutes.

My ex, Jep, was out front, waving his arms for us to go on around back, by the south alley. Some people stood in their front yards with binoculars, dressed in nothing but housedresses and hairnets. A group of hunters that had been dropping off their animals for mounting when the bear came around were helping to direct traffic, even though there was none. When we parked the truck and got out, one of the hunters, wearing camo and neon orange tape weaved into the braid down his back, approached us to let us know that they were fully prepared to provide backup, fire arsenal and all, if needed. We declined the offer and walked down the east wall of the building and around the corner to the Dumpster, located out back, where Jep deposited the guts and brains and other parts of the animals he didn't need to stuff people's trophies. Let's just say the taxidermy Dumpster put off a strong venisony odor that a bear might be attracted to the way some women were attracted across department stores to the perfume section.

The bear was inside the Dumpster, eating and sort of talking to himself. Mack banged on the metal wall with the toe of his steel-toed boot, and the bear's head appeared. The faces of bears, once you're used to looking at them, are expressive, each one singular and his own. He was an adult bear, but only just. His fur was matted along his shoulder blades and showed no normal sheen or luster. The tip of his left ear was missing in a half-moon bite. Who knows where it came from—a battle with a mountain lion or with his own father, or frostbite; it could have been any number of things. His nose lacked shine, a sign of poor health. The smell of him was powerful, as if he'd been rolling in fish heads and dirty socks, and it wasn't just all the garbage he'd been wallowing in recently. Mostly he just smelled like a pungent male bear. He was the biggest black bear I'd ever laid eyes on in my six years on the job.

Although I never would have admitted it at the time, for months I was afraid to get out of the cab of my truck and face the forest, look it in the eye. I'd park somewhere where none of the other Division of Wildlife agents would come across me and eat potato chips, my eyes glazed over. The only thought I allowed myself was: Girl, what in the hell were you thinking, going into wildlife biology? The fact of the matter was that it was easier than getting through veterinary school. And I could live in Point-of-the-Rocks, the small town where I grew up in the deserted windy valley bordering Wyoming but technically inside Colorado. I always thought I loved animals. Kittens and horses and the tame scratch-behind-the-ears type. I didn't have a repugnance for spiders or snakes, and I watched a lot of Discovery Channel.

Which didn't help me now. All the noise and over-stimulated voices from the street made the bear swivel his ears nervously. Mack indicated we should overturn the Dumpster if we were able by prying it over with a crowbar. I jogged back to the truck for the metal bar while Mack baby-talked him. Sweet talk can work on bruins the way it works on pets. Sometimes a bear will roll over and grin like a dog when you call. But this bear was in a pickle, cornered with people everywhere, no escape. I decided we needed to disperse the crowd.

Jep was sitting on the hood of his car out front. He was wearing his gore-stained work apron and the knee-high moccasins we'd bought him that summer we took off and drove to the Grand Canyon. We'd bought the moccasins at one of those booths along the highway, crossing the Navajo reservation, where they sold jewelry and kachina dolls. Back then it had been us, we, *nosotros*. The collective pronoun used to be something I thought of mostly in terms of Jep and me, me and Jep. I'd never seen the end coming, and then there it was. Put into simple words over dinner plates. It had taken as much concentration to translate those simple words as if they had been in ancient Hebrew or something. Jep, my Jep, telling me he wanted to move out of our house.

"Do you know what *taxidermy* means, the parts of the word?" he'd asked me that night.

"No," I'd answered with a sigh. "What?" Jep had a thing about looking words up in the dictionary for their Latin derivatives.

"*Taxis* is a surgical term meaning the replacement by hand of some displaced part without cutting any tissue. And *dermy* refers to skin. What you do for a living is manage and manipulate nature, and what I do is capture its form indefinitely, minus its soul. What kind of way is this to make a buck? The emptiness starts to take over, you know?"

I had always known Jep had some discomfort about his profession. He had taken over the family business when his father had let it slide nearly into bankruptcy. "What I want to know is how you feel."

"I feel … like I'm disappearing. This is a hard place to live, you know that? Seven months of winter. Yeah, we've got blue herons and antelope and whatever else. But it's a hard way of life. That's why everyone is always leaving here."

"I'm not leaving," I'd said. But he was already rounding up the dishes and filling the sink with water.

"I'd just like to do one thing right, one thing that puts me a part of … whatever." He hadn't finished his sentence, started talking nonsense about selling off the taxidermy business to buy an island in the Sea of Cortez. We'd washed the dishes, me and Jep, the last thing we'd done as a *we,* and went to bed, and in the morning, while I was at work, he'd moved into a storage space in the back of his taxidermy shop.

◈

I grabbed the crowbar out of the back of the Wildlife truck and, as I jogged past him, I said, "Hey, Jep, you mind getting the sheriff over here to disperse these people?"

He nodded, one polite tip of his chin, and went inside without a word or a look.

By the time I got back around the building with the crowbar, Mack had the bear out of the Dumpster already. He'd made him mad enough to lunge out of the box, swatting his massive paws, and tip himself over. The bear batted at Mack from a crouched position against the metal siding of the building. When I came around the corner, the animal's eyes rolled in my direction briefly, and I read the expression of bravado in his look. Bravado to cover up the terror and the healthy dose of embarrassment. No animal reacts to humans circling with guns the same way. We wildlife agents don't talk about this part of the job. It's just understood.

"I'm gonna back off your direction," Mack said. "And then we're going to herd him down the hill toward the river. Okay?"

"Yeah," I said. My hand was on the handle of my gun. We'd both loaded our guns with rubber bullets. I could hear the sheriff's voice in the street behind us, rounding people up and moving them away.

"Look there, now, see how nice I am?" Mack said, baby-talking the bear. "Now, whoa there, big boy. Nobody's playing any trick or treats here. See my cute little pink hands? I'm just going to—" He backed off until he was at my side. Mack didn't like to use the cattle prod, and we'd only shoot the rubber bullets if that was what we had to do.

Even with the glitter of shame buried in his eyes, the bear held his head and shoulders regally. It was like trying to shoo Napoleon. He was a kingly animal, born to inherit the shadows of the forest. I liked him, and I was sorry to be without any better language to tell him so. Sorry I was a woman and he was a trespassing black bear.

We started toward him, Mack using the crowbar to poke him in the butt. The bear reared up to full height. He sent the metal bar twirling over our heads like a baton into a neighbor's yard. It was like seeing a piano falling on you from ten stories up.

"Fire," Mack commanded, and, from no more than fifteen feet away, we each fired once, aiming at the bear's haunches and mostly firing for noise. The animal retracted, thrown back against the wall. He gathered himself up instantly and, on all fours, hunkered fast, limping on a back leg where he'd been hit in the rump, over the hill into the junkyards.

We followed to be sure he kept going and that he wasn't hurt and that he didn't veer across the highway into town. He didn't. We tracked him over two miles up Yellow Jacket Creek until we were sure he'd made it onto federal lands, and then we called it good enough and went home.

◆

Three days later, the bear turned up dead, shot through the heart with an arrow.

A rancher was the one to discover the carcass and call the sheriff, who then notified us. The rancher leased the grazing rights on the stretch of public lands along the river. He claimed he'd been moving his cattle up meadow when he happened to spot the dark shape in the willows.

Mack sent me out to look things over. I followed the directions the rancher had given the sheriff. It took me a half hour of stomping around along the river bottom before I found the bear's body, on its side in a fetal position, as if curled around the fatal wound in its breast. The orange and green arrow lay close by, torn from the flesh with the dexterous hand of the bear himself.

It was a cold morning. The bank clock in town had reported the temperature at negative five degrees Fahrenheit. It was cold enough to spring tears to the eyes and freeze them in the lashes. The bear lay on the bank of the river on a peninsula of earth formed between an old frozen oxbow and the river. Nearby, the river flowed over a deserted beaver dam, ice coating every twig and branch in a white cascade. The half moon was still up and appeared coldly in the blue sky above the red of the bare willows. I got down on a knee and touched the bear's face. The carcass was too frozen to tell how long it had lain there. The eyes were closed but still, the expression of bravado remained somehow. There was a lot of blood everywhere, frozen now all over the animal's torso and neck and staining the brittle grass around him, as if the arrow had only grazed the heart and the cause of death had been loss of blood.

I searched around for tracks. I figured the ones with the deep heel were the rancher's cowboy boots. The cattle had been let out on the river bottom, and their trampling had stomped out most other traces of the bear's killer. I knew Mack wouldn't advise a thorough search. It would only be a thousand-dollar fine for poaching the bear, and it was hunting season. Mack needed me out in the high country, checking for tagged kills as the hunters broke down their camps and left. But I spent a good hour and a half looking around for any other tracks that might have survived the cattle trampling. I don't know why. I was sorry about the bear's death. I finally found something in the frozen mud along the river, maybe two hundred feet upstream from the carcass. I stared at the print. It didn't make sense.

It was a naked human footprint.

◈

Mack was the one who talked to the rancher. He was our first suspect. He had a motive. No rancher wants a starving bear skulking around on his grazing lease with his yearlings. But Mack said it was clear after five minutes talking with the man that stumbling across the dead bear had been a big shock for him. Not that the rancher was any sort of softy. But he didn't carry a rifle in his pickup or when he was on the range. The rancher was disgusted with how low the fine was for poaching a bear. He was a man of about sixty-five with an overgrown, yellowing mustache and hearing aids that he fidgeted with. He recalled the days of his grandfather's youth when seeing a bear wasn't something that happened once in your life but was a regular occurrence that marked your day. "Back in those days," the rancher said, "bear meat was worth something. You couldn't just go out and buy these *tubes* of hamburger at the grocery. You could feed a family half a winter on a bear that size. Waste of meat, this kind of poaching. I'd like to see whoever done it spend a night in the jailhouse. But that's my opinion. Suppose you people got a book you do things by."

◈

In the middle of the night, unable to sleep without Jep in bed beside me, I got up and called the number at the taxidermy shop, but there was no answer except the answering machine. He hadn't been returning my calls, so I didn't bother leaving a message. I sat up and drank a mug of warm milk, waiting to be tired and reading the classifieds in the back of the newspaper, dreaming of jobs that don't haunt you with visions of arrogant black bears bled to death on the banks of rivers.

Finally, I got back under the covers and stared at the ceiling, but I couldn't stop thinking about the bear on the riverbank. Who would do such a thing? Track a bear down and put an arrow in his heart? Maybe, I thought, someone who'd been at the taxidermy shop the day we scared him off with rubber bullets. Like the hunters who'd offered their services that day. I told myself I would check it out tomorrow. If they hadn't left the state yet.

◈

The next day, early, I made my out-of-state phone calls to the hunters while Mack and one of the other wildlife guys, Joe Creek, went out and loaded the bear up and delivered him to the local supermarket to be skinned and processed. It would be a couple days, the butcher told them, with the high volume of work they had coming in with hunting season, but that's what they had freezer lockers for. When they got back to the station, we talked over whether or not the hunters might have done the poaching.

"They seemed sincerely surprised by the news when I talked to them on the phone," I told Mack. "And why would they be dragging their archery equipment out here for a rifle season all the way from"—I checked my notes—"North Dakota?"

"Maybe it was someone else at the taxidermy place that day," Mack said. "Maybe it was a local."

"Hey," Joe Creek said, popping his head up from under the computer desk where he was trying to install some new equipment. "Did you get that message out by the phone?"

"Who, me?" I said.

"Yeah. Some guy named Rattlesnake? Do you know anyone by that name?"

"Yeah. He's Jep's technical assistant at the taxidermy shop. Worked for him forever."

"Why's he called Rattlesnake?"

"I don't know. It's just what he's called. He's an Apache from Arizona, and I guess he's famous for doing the finest job of stuffing snakes. So what'd he say?"

"Something about, have you seen Jep lately. He hasn't been into the shop for a few days."

"Not even to sleep? That's where he's living."

"I guess not."

"Maybe he took a vacation without telling anybody."

"Could be. But he'd have to have hitchhiked."

"Why?"

"His van is still parked out back."

◈

Three days Jep had been gone. And three days since someone had sent an arrow zinging into the rib cage of the black bear. It seemed funny to me. After work, I went over to the taxidermy shop and talked to Rattlesnake, a little old man who always wore his shirt buttoned to the throat and always carried a book in his back pocket, usually a Western but sometimes a True Crime. He had no social graces, a pure recluse, and here he was running the place alone. He was listening to Paul Harvey on the radio and organizing the glass eyes by size and color.

"Still haven't heard from Jep?" I asked.

The old man shook his head, slow and solemn, like an old trout finding its way up current.

"Maybe he left a note somewhere."

"Nope," Rattlesnake said.

"Maybe it got lost in the shuffle."

Again, the slow shake of the head.

"What if I look around a bit."

"Okay."

In Jep's office, I checked the desk and the floor under it for a note or some scrap of info that might tell me where Jep had gotten off to. Then I checked his answering machine. One message was from me, about a week ago, sounding whiney, but there was nothing else. I wandered back to the storage room where Jep had a bed and dresser and alarm clock set up. I sat on his saggy cot of a bed and looked around the small room at his belongings, his world. The bird identification poster over his dresser. A potted cactus on the windowsill. A stack of books: *Teach Yourself to Speak Spanish Fluently!* and other Spanish home-course guides. Jep had always wanted to visit Mexico but didn't want to go unless he spoke the language. Maybe that's where he was—Mexico. We had planned to go together, but my two-week vacation time wasn't sufficient for Jep. I was too scared to quit my job, too scared to keep it. And Jep didn't help. He wanted to disappear into Mexico with nothing to come home for. This was always how he'd talk about such ideas. You wouldn't know it by looking at him—successful, small-town business owner with a wry smile and a sexy, relaxed way of leaning back in a chair—but he was a dreamer. And it's the nature of all dreamers that they live perpetually on the rocky shores of disappointment.

I noticed a bookmark in a book of Spanish poems and removed it. He had underlined a few lines of the poem "Oh Earth, Wait for Me" by Pablo Neruda. It was a disturbing passage, and there was something in the heavy-handed underlining that made me wonder at his reasons for picking this poem out from among the others. There was one line in particular I didn't understand—how could someone go back to being something they have not been?

I put the book quickly back where I found it. So as not to bother Rattlesnake, I left by the back exit. I only thought to look around Jep's work shed out back as an afterthought.

I turned on an overhead light bulb and right away spotted the tatters of orange and green feathers and other materials flung across his workbench, left behind after he'd used them to build arrows.

◈

I made some phone calls. One to Jep's mother, who had moved to Arizona with a second husband, and another to his father, who drove a truck and was gone a lot. Neither had heard from Jep. There was nothing much I (as his ex-girlfriend) or we (the Division of Wildlife) could do. It was a thousand-dollar fine that could wait until he turned up. *If* he turned up. His room hadn't looked ransacked, as if he'd packed in a hurry, or even as if anything were missing. And anyway, what reason did he have to shoot a bear through the heart? This was the question that went with me everywhere as I continued to carry out the duties of my job and what was left of my life. No one knew Jep better than I did. I wasn't just thinking that because I was a jilted girlfriend. I tried to be honest about the facts. I mean, obviously, I loved him. I loved the finer points about him. The way his hair looked as if he'd been licked all over by a cat in the morning. How when I was sick he nursed me back to health with strange garlicky herb soups and bedtime stories from *The Field Guide to Insects and Spiders*. How he preferred his own cooking to mine. How he looked when he laughed good and hard, which was plenty, and how he looked when he was sad, which was plenty, too. Maybe he didn't love me. But you could have fooled me for four solid years. I remember how it felt to turn into his embrace in the early morning hours and find him waiting for me to wake. His full attention zoomed in on me. His breath, his hands, his skin, everything about him awake to me.

◈

I don't know when it was—a week after the black bear took the arrow? More? The supermarket that was processing the animal called to have us come in. Mack and I went together, thinking we'd need both sets of arms to carry the hide and the boxes of meat to the truck. But when the butcher brought us back to his meat lockers, we found the bear still in one piece, lying on the butcher's block like a patient under deep anesthesia, his massive paws dangling off the table, palms up but stiff, in a state of rigor mortis or thaw. The animal had been cut open, and along a seam down its middle, the flesh could be seen, pinkly, inside.

"I called you in to have a look at this," the butcher said, wiping his hands down the front of his apron. He pulled the folds of the bear's hide back. I had seen denuded bears before, and I knew what they looked like: very similar to a burn victim, human in shape and stature but raw. This carcass was smooth.

The butcher reached up into the folds and lifted away more of the hide so we could see that inside was no animal carcass but the body of a human being. The blood was the bear's, but the face was one I recognized. I recognized the expression of the mouth, the set of the jaw, the deep-set eyes, closed and sunken as if in restless sleep. But this was no sleep. Jep's arms fit as if into sleeves inside the animal's front legs. His legs fit into the animal's back legs as if into a roomy pair of pants. I backed away, the sound of my own blood throbbing behind my ears.

The butcher was saying, "There was a split up the front of the animal when you brought him in. Must be how he removed the bear's skeleton. Of course, he knew what he was doing, taxidermist and all. I imagine the rest of the animal will turn up one of these days. Along with his clothes. Maybe he buried it all. The body was still frozen when you brought him in, which, I reckon, kept everything together. I don't know. I been sitting here puzzling over it all morning. I never seen nothing like it."

"No," Mack was saying. "Jesus. I wonder what his cause of death was. You find any bullet wounds?"

"Nope. Nothing. And, believe me, I thought to look," the butcher said. "Suppose we ought to give the sheriff a call?"

"Yeah," Mack said. "Yeah."

I seemed to hear them up a chimney, darkly and somewhere far above me. I stared at Jep, his face looking out from inside the bear, and it's hard to explain how I felt. I felt as if I were looking into that forest I was never able to look directly at, only now I had to. Everything beautiful and wild and unsaid lay opened up at its seams to reveal its carnage. I remembered the footprint in the frozen mud on the banks of the river, and I could see him. Naked, crouching to wash the blood off his arms, then wading in to the waist, then deeper, heart level and then under, unfeeling of the bitter cold as he waited for the hypothermia to set in and make him numb. He would have felt the sensation of the broken triangles of ice swiveling past him. Waiting for the imaginary warmth to ooze through his bloodstream and then the sleepiness to call him to his bed. To see him so clearly when all along I was unable to see him for what he was. It was never me. Why couldn't I hear him when he said he was disappearing? All I could see was my own disappearance.

I think I was crying. I think I was holding the bear's head, cradling it against myself. I looked down into the bear's face and called it by my lover's name.

Miriam's Lantern

Ray Keifetz

"Under a spreading chestnut tree / the village smithy stands."
— Henry Wadsworth Longfellow

Chestnut trees really did shade the town where I learned to smith. My father apprenticed me after having read in some journal that the outlook for wagons and carriages had never been brighter. Henry Ford had just introduced the Model T, but that detail was overlooked by the journal. Also overlooked was what happened that afternoon in a nearby field.

That summer afternoon, while my father sat on the porch reading his journal, I went into the field with my two cousins and our three shotguns. We fired at whatever hopped, or fluttered, or cheeped—wrens, meadowlarks, redwing blackbirds. I saw a bird I had never seen before: small, gray-blue, and very round. I saw it in my sights. What a neat bird, I thought and squeezed the trigger. I carried it home by its feet. My father, putting down his journal, said, Good shot, son. I didn't think there were any left.

Thus began my long apprenticeship. I learned to smelt

and temper, cast and hammer, by the colors of fire—the ripe orange orange, the blinding yellow white, the deep ruby so like the eyes of that small dead bird. With every blow my arms grew stronger, the hammer lighter. Not only iron, my master said, we forge ourselves. So do we temper. Shoes by the hundreds, by the thousands, bits and bridles and fittings—shackles I now know—but how beautiful and worthy I thought them then of the beasts they constrained. The shoeing—how fast could you take the flat stock and match it to a hoof? Our world rang with bells of bone and iron. Wooden wagons, carts, and carriages, drawn by the great horses our hard hands had shod, streamed down the winding roads in an unstoppable flood. I was fast and strong, getting faster and stronger, and one afternoon I shouted, Bring on more work. I'm waiting—

I must have given offense. McAuliff the journeyman put down his hammer and crossed his arms. They were the width of chestnut limbs.

"What kind of fool are you, Marner, that you can't see?"

"I guess I can see as good as the next."

"Then why can't you see it ain't you that's gotten faster. It's the work that's gotten slower."

My route to work took me down an aisle of chestnut trees. These great trees shaded us in summer, fed us in the fall; their wood upon which dampness had scant effect timbered our barns and fenced our fields year round. My eagerness to reach the forge, the flames, turned my way into a green, leafy blur. But a few days after offending the journeyman, I saw something that made me stop and stare. Maybe it was the falling leaves swirling sluggishly in the muggy air. Maybe it was the season—high summer and green everywhere—and that these leaves falling in clouds were dry and brown. I looked up. The entire crown was ablaze but without a single nut pod, which ripen and fall before the leaves. As I resumed my walk, the far side of the trunk came into view. The rough bark was bloated with lumps and giant boils, split open with long vertical fissures dripping orange dust. I rushed from tree to tree, circled each trunk, looked up, looked down … some of them still appeared as if they might stand forever, but everywhere else the cracks, the boils, the orange dust …

When I reached the forge I said to McAuliff, "There's something happening to the trees!"

He said, "That is the least of your worries."

I stared at him and made another discovery. The journeyman's hair was gray. McAuliff had become an old man. Then I looked at the forge. Where were the flames? I threw on more wood, worked the bellows. The yellow flames leaped. Then I heard the master calling my name and McAuliff saying better not keep him waiting.

The master was sitting behind his table—a log he'd split to test the edge of an axe and planed smooth. He was counting out some bills and coins. Without looking up he said, "Marner, I'm letting you go."

"After all these years—without a hint—without a warning—"

"Hint? Warning? Haven't you eyes?"

"It don't seem right."

"It ain't right," he said, pushing the money toward me.

"All these years—" was what I said.

"You're still young," was what he answered.

◈

It was the earliest autumn anyone could remember and for countless chestnut trees the last. They just flared up in a burst of brilliant color and died. The same also for many a forge and foundry. My first stop a group of men were sitting in front of a cold hearth, their arms enormous from when they still fed it.

"I'm looking for work."

"You find any, you let us know."

Before my eyes their great bare forearms began to swell and crack . . . I looked again and they were as before, dangling uselessly by their sides.

The road out of town was not the one I had come in on. Automobiles racing round the turns pushed me and the few remaining horse carts, drivers, and horses choking into the brush. Almost a journeyman, I went from town to town climbing hills, dipping into hollows, searching for work. But everywhere the fires were dying. When I started my apprenticeship, it was as though the stars in the sky for want of room had come down onto the hilltops and into the hollows between, so many stars twinkling up there and down here, and now it seemed as if half the sky had been snuffed out. I walked through groves of dead chestnut trees, their limbs lying shattered in the dust. Here and there I'd come to a sapling shooting up, pencil-thin in a race against the blistering rust. One solitary fruit was now all they could bear, just enough to forward the agony.

Once in a long while I'd find a forge or foundry not yet snuffed and inquire after work. Experience? they'd ask, and I would tell them proudly that I was almost a journeyman. The first man said, and he more or less spoke for the few that followed, "I was kind of looking for someone without his way of doing so there'd be room to take in my way of doing."

"I can learn," I said.

"Not on my time."

Early winter followed early fall, and spring was belated. I found work sharpening lawn mower blades and straightening bicycle frames. Puttering and sputtering at this and that I would hear, as if he were standing right behind me, my master's voice, and I would repeat out loud his scornful words—*you call yourself a smith*—and pack up and move on.

Then I heard a rumor of a town deep in the woods that the blight had not yet reached, a town still needing a smith. The town—Praywell, strange name—seemed in truth the answer to my prayers. Chestnut trees ripe with fruit, their trunks strong and sound, shaded a narrow street lined with the workshops of potters, spinners, weavers, glass blowers, turners, and joiners. At the very end, just before the street turned back into the woods, stood an abandoned blacksmith shop, its forge gone out and cold. I told them I had no money, given even the shape the place was in, to buy it. They said you don't have to buy it, just light it and keep it lit, keep the forge burning. Here is all the flat stock you will need for shoes, iron enough to shoe a herd, rasps enough to bevel the world … But where, I asked, are my customers, my farmers and carriage makers—

"Gone," they said. "Surely you have seen … "

I said no more. For there were anvils and hammers, and my arms were strong. There was a loft, warm and tight, and my body ached from the nights on the ground. Thus resumed my long apprenticeship. Hour after hour I hammered out shoes no horse would ever wear and at the end of the day thrust them back into the flames, day after day starting anew what I had destroyed the night before. Separated by a sagging rope, I'd explain to the infrequent visitors down from the city the colors of fire—the ripe orange orange, the blinding yellow white, the deep ruby so like the eyes of a small dead bird—explaining to the indifference beyond the rope what my life had been reduced to.

The last visitor had left hours ago, and the shadows pressed against me when I heard a woman's voice:

"So how does it feel to be a piece of living history?"

I turned and saw a woman standing at the rope, her face glowing in the forge light. Her hair streaked with gray, she looked careworn but at the same time almost young, youthful.

"If you call it living," I answered.

"I do," she said and wished me good night.

Every morning as I worked the bellows, I'd watch for her walking past my open doors on the way to the meadow outside of town, and I would watch for her return hours later, wicker baskets overflowing with roots and flowers. And all afternoon as I tended my own fire I'd think of her, of Miriam tending her fires, her kettles boiling, her dyes spreading. In the evening when the last horseshoes had been melted flat, cooled and stacked, I would walk up and down Praywell's only street, my booted feet thumping the wooden planks, crickets singing in the trees. Back and forth from one end of town to the other I paced, passing the closed doors of joiners and weavers and spinners, passing the dyer's door, Miriam's. One evening as I approached her door for maybe the fourth time I saw that her light was still burning, a warm, inviting light that spilled through the cracks and formed a glowing pool at my feet. I knocked softly. Miriam opened and let me in.

"I'm working late," she said.

"But what is the point?" I said. "What we make goes nowhere."

"Nowhere?"

"I forge a hundred horseshoes only to melt them down again."

"And Matthew planes a hundred cherrywood boards. And planes them again. Lucy spins her thread from the skein she unraveled yesterday—"

"What futility!"

"Tell that to the nest-building birds, to the spiders, the beavers, the ants … tell that to the weavers and spinners and builders of the earth—"

"But those are animals."

"Yes," Miriam said. "They are."

Miriam continued stirring her dye. I peered into the kettle

and saw our faces coming close together and the lantern above rippling back from the dark indigo.

"Sometimes," I said, "it feels like a punishment."

She kept stirring, and I kept peering.

"A man apprentices himself for seven years, a man with arms like these, and he can't find a job. How can the world be so wide and have no room for a pair of skillful hands?"

"There is room," she said. "Maybe not very much. Tucked away off to the side and in the far corners, you can still find some."

From then on I tried to work as if I had no mind, no aspirations, neither past nor future, as if the hammer, iron, and my arms were one, as if they had as much choice to rise and fall as my heart to beat. What is mastery anyway, Miriam had said, but a kind of forgetting? Day followed identical day, my speed increasing, my arms broadening. Whenever doubt darkened me, I would glance in on Miriam. Her faith, her acceptance, was a lantern whose light illuminated the vague outlines of a path, which her smile invited me to follow.

As I was working the bellows one day, explaining the flames to a young couple behind the rope, I heard the young man whisper to the girl: "It's like going to the zoo."

After they left I barred the doors and extinguished the forge. On the way out of town I stopped by Miriam's door to say good-bye.

"I can't stay here any longer."

"But why?"

"Look at my arms—" I held them out to her. "Look how they've withered."

The world was wide, after all. Why was I hiding like some criminal in a far corner? I went up to the city to try my luck. You can always find work in a city, particularly if you swallow your pride.

Two blocks from the city zoo I found a room. I soon

learned that it was in this very zoo, in the woods surrounding the caged animals, that the first blighted chestnut was discovered. At the earliest opportunity I paid a visit to see for myself the source of the contagion. That tree, however, had long since been felled: only its stump, wide enough to dance upon, remained ringed by sickly shoots. Though I had no further interest here, I nevertheless continued onward, compelled, it almost felt, by someone or something calling to me in distress. Up ahead a group of boys was jeering at a curious, shaggy beast pacing back and forth in its cage. At my approach they moved on. The harmless-seeming creature—singular, sterile, the sign said, its ferocious parents having been of different but closely related species—gave a soft growl and continued its interminable pacing. I wandered off the main road with its cages and pools and came to a brick building. There were no cages here. Instead a flock of fluttering leaflets pinned to a board offered employment opportunities. And as I had already passed the elephant house and seen the men going about with their shovels, I went in without reading further.

The man behind the desk looked as tired and faded as his brown suit. His name, Mr. Kearney—Irish, I supposed. He asked me if I liked animals. I told him how, before commencing my apprenticeship, I had worked on a farm. He said I asked you if you liked animals. I miss the wagons, I said, the carriages. I miss them because of the horses and not just because I made my living from them, but for the sound of their hooves, the sparks flying …

"What about birds?"

"I sure miss those horses."

"I'm asking you about birds."

"There used to be some. In the trees. There used to be some trees." Shaking his head, Mr. Kearney stood up, and I did the same. After all, there were plenty of other jobs in the city …

"You may work out," he said. "Because if you cared a jot,

you wouldn't last an hour."

A chilling drizzle, typical of this city, had begun to fall. I followed Mr. Kearney past a line of shivering people.

"Some days there's nobody here," Mr. Kearney said. "Then some newspaperman happens to remember, writes a story ... "

I glanced at the faces of the men and women—what were they hoping to find up ahead?—while Mr. Kearney went on about the fickleness of human beings, how they never seemed to care about anything until the situation was past caring, as for instance the passing of beings other than themselves, by which I understood him to mean animals but of whom he spoke with reverence, as if their presence or absence among us were on a par with heaven and our future therein. From these remarks, and from the hundreds of people waiting patiently in the miserable weather, I concluded that something huge and splendid must be dying.

At a nod from Mr. Kearney, a uniformed guard announced that the building was closed and that all were welcome to return tomorrow. We had it to ourselves, the dark, deserted interior in which a lone cylindrical mesh cage illuminated by a single spotlight's downward beam occupied the center.

"Take a good look, Marner. In my lifetime their migrations darkened the sky. Take a good look. For now and forever, you're looking at the last of them."

Even before he spoke I had already recognized the small bluish bird against whose eyes I gauged my fires—

"There were millions of them once," he said. "As recent as fifteen years ago, so-called sportsmen were still organizing shoots. As recent as ten years ago, boys with guns were popping them out of trees. I ask you, Marner, can such people be forgiven?"

The bird swiveled its head and fixed me with its blood-red eye.

"No," I whispered. "And they should not be."

We stayed in that dark room for hours, staring and breathing. I felt Mr. Kearney beside me, his outrage, his pity. I felt, as with myself, that he could not remove his eyes from the small bird perched alone on a dowel. I kept waiting for Mr. Kearney to raise his voice, to shout down the shotgun blasts reverberating through the aviary, but he must have been waiting for me to do the same.

"What do you want of me?"

"It's very simple," he answered. "I want you to watch."

◈

I was issued a uniform and instructed to keep back the crowds, though a slack rope suspended between opposite walls would have sufficed. Most of the time there were no crowds, only a hungry, waiting silence, which I tried to keep back as well. Day after day I watched the bird whose solitude could not be measured. The passing of an entire race, Mr. Kearney said, must not go unnoticed. Can't you see the multitudes, the whirling dark clouds, the endless blue light, the generations fluttering and breathing because this lone individual continues to breathe and flutter? I saw only a small solitary bird, a small solitary ending that took red berries from my hand. Its bluish head swiveling iridescently from side to side—what did it see? Day and night I brooded on letting the bird go. Together the two of us, of unrelated but closely connected species, from separate but closely related cages, would rise up into the sky—

Not a day passed without Mr. Kearney looking in.

"When nothing else is left," he said, "there's the waiting."

The bird sidled down its dowel toward Mr. Kearney.

"It knows you," I said.

"These birds mate for life. They're not meant to be alone."

"Maybe another will turn up."

"The last one turned up about nine years ago on a kitchen pile—a few bones, a few feathers, a lot of buckshot."

"Maybe in some far-off spot—"

"Where?"

"Some tucked-away spot," I said, "where boys don't carry guns." And I started to cough.

The cough got worse; my breath rattled through the darkness, but the nature of my work forbade me to miss a single day. Even on my days off you would find me leaning over the guardrail, eyes fixed on the tiny bird perched behind the mesh. I asked Mr. Kearney how old did he guess the bird to be; what age did he expect the bird to reach? It was hard to say, Mr. Kearney said. It seemed a healthy specimen.

And yet I sensed that beneath its soft plush plumage, as with me beneath my sweat-stiff uniform, the plump little bird was slowly withering. Slowly, irrevocably, but with a hearty appetite. Day after day I fed it the red berries that it loved and watched. I watched and waited, my ragged breath filling the dark room. And the tiny bird gazed back at me and at whomever else was there or not there, at all of us, the present and absent with equal equanimity as if presence or absence beyond the mesh could not have the slightest impact on the greater absence within.

Every morning, covered in sweat from a night of not sleeping, I would rush from my room to the wire mesh whose sign in the language of verdicts declared NO OTHERS ARE KNOWN—lest that verdict be commuted in my absence to NONE ... I lost all sense of days, months, years, the difference between, between a day and a year, a moment and a lifetime; there were only days now, only one day really—

And then I woke to a strange stillness. The shotguns had ceased their blasting. I seemed to see my face as if reflected in a deep well, and beside my face, almost touching, the dyer Miriam's—and from these signs I understood that *the day* had come.

Wheezing, scarcely able to breathe, I rushed to the cage. But there the bluish bird sat as usual upon its thin perch, unchanged, unchanging, swiveling its head in my direction as I pitched forward toward its feet.

It was Mr. Kearney who found me at the foot of the cage, my fingers wrapped around a handful of red berries, and shook me awake. For a moment the two of us crouched there together on the cold cement floor, the light from above, a light so familiar, so soothing, cascading down on us, bathing us in radiance. I lifted my eyes and for an instant beheld in this glimmering true light not only the one last bird but all the birds, the multitudes in swirling flight, the nest builders, weavers … other creatures as well, the diggers, burrowers, the builders of this earth who do their work without cease or complaint.

Mr. Kearney helped me to my feet, but it was not only Mr. Kearney. The cage was brilliantly illuminated, and the little bird clearly perched within, yet flapping his short stubby wings, he seemed to be helping me up, too, as if somehow he had managed to enter my cage or I had fallen into his.

"I was wrong about you, Marner," Mr. Kearney said. "You do care."

I was hoping I would die first. "I was trying … "

Soon after, Mr. Kearney let me go. It was a kindness.

I packed a rucksack with food—bags full of red berries and for myself dry bread, hard cheese—and set out for the hills and hollows, the woods and open fields of my childhood. The countryside had become even darker, as if somewhere the dikes and sandbags had all collapsed, and I made my way as through a dark flood. Yet my heart was buoyant, for perhaps this darkness had to be if I were to pick out the faint glimmering, the unassuming radiance of Miriam's lantern and by its light take up again, for now and forever, my unfinished apprenticeship.

Contributors

Mary Akers is the author of two short story collections, *Bones of an Inland Sea* (Press 53, 2013) and *Women Up On Blocks* (Press 53, 2009), and the nonfiction book *One Life to Give* (The Experiment, 2010). She is editor-in-chief of the online journal *r.kv.r.y.* and has been a VCCA Fellow and a Bread Loaf waiter. She co-founded the Institute for Tropical Marine Ecology, a study abroad marine ecology program originally located in Roseau, Dominica. Akers frequently writes fiction that focuses on the intersections between art and science, including such topics as diverse and timely as the environmental movement and the struggle for human and animal rights. Although raised in the Blue Ridge Mountains of Virginia, which she will always call home, she currently lives in western New York.

Philip Armstrong is the co-director of the New Zealand Center for Human-Animal Studies at the University of Canterbury in Christchurch (www.nzchas.canterbury.ac.nz). His most recent scholarly book is *What Animals Mean in the Fiction of Modernity* (Routledge, 2008). He has published short fiction and poetry in various journals and anthologies in New Zealand and Australia.

Sara Dupree is a Ph.D. candidate at the University of North Dakota, where she has received the John Little Award for fiction and the Thomas McGrath Award for poetry. She lives in Grand Forks with her husband, two daughters, two dogs, two cats, and two horses. Her work has appeared in *Conclave* and *Alligator Juniper.*

Melodie Edwards graduated with an MFA from the University of Michigan on a Colby Fellowship, where she received two Hopwood Awards in fiction and nonfiction. *Glimmer Train* published "Si-Si-Gwa-D" in 2002, one of the winners of their New Writers fiction contest. She has published stories in *South Dakota Quarterly, North Dakota Review, Michigan Quarterly, Prairie Schooner,* and others. A nature essay, "A Lament for My Jacobson's Organ," received first prize in *Crazyhorse*'s nonfiction contest. In 2005, she received the Doubleday Wyoming Arts Council Award for Women. "The Bird Lady" aired on NPR's Selected Shorts and was nominated for a Pushcart Prize. She lives in Laramie, Wyoming, with her husband and twin daughters and co-owns Night Heron Books and Coffeehouse.

Carol Guess is the author of eleven books of poetry and prose, including *Switch, Tinderbox Lawn*, and *Doll Studies: Forensics.* Forthcoming books include *How To Feel Confident With Your Special Talents* (co-written with Daniela Olszewska) and *X Marks The Dress: A Registry* (co-written with Kristina Marie Darling). She is professor of English at Western Washington University, where she teaches creative writing and queer studies.

Patrick Hicks is the author of five poetry collections, most recently *Finding the Gossamer* and *This London*. He is also the editor of *A Harvest of Words*, which was funded by the National

Endowment for the Humanities. His work has appeared in *Ploughshares, Glimmer Train, The Missouri Review, Tar River Poetry, New Ohio Review, Salon, Prairie Schooner, Natural Bridge,* and many others. He has been nominated seven times for the Pushcart Prize and was recently a finalist for the High Plains Book Award, the Dzanc Short Story Collection Competition, and the Gival Press Novel Award. He has won the *Glimmer Train* Fiction Award and received grants from the Bush Foundation and the South Dakota Arts Council. In 2014, his poetry collection *Adoptable* will be published by Salmon Poetry, and his first novel, *The Commandant of Lubizec,* will be published by Steerforth/Random House. In 2015, his short story collection, *The Collector of Names,* will be published by Schaffner Press. He is the writer-in-residence at Augustana College as well as a faculty member at the low-residency MFA program at Sierra Nevada College.

Julian Hoffman lives beside the Prespa Lakes in northern Greece, monitoring birds in upland areas where wind farms have been built or proposed. His book, *The Small Heart of Things: Being at Home in a Beckoning World,* was chosen by Terry Tempest Williams as the winner of the 2012 AWP Award Series for creative nonfiction and was published in 2013. Along with winning the 2011 *Terrain.org* Nonfiction Prize, his work has appeared in *Kyoto Journal, Southern Humanities Review, EarthLines, Cold Mountain Review,* and *Flyway,* among others. You can catch up with Julian at www.julian-hoffman.com.

Suzanne Kamata is the author of the novels *Gadget Girl: The Art of Being Invisible* (GemmaMedia, 2013) and *Losing Kei* (Leapfrog Press, 2008), as well as a short story collection, *The Beautiful One Has Come* (Wyatt-Mackenzie Publishing, 2011). She is also the editor of three anthologies. Her essays and short stories have appeared in more than 100 publications, including *Real Simple; Brain, Child; The Utne Reader*; *Crab Orchard Review;* and *Calyx*. She currently serves as fiction editor of *Kyoto Journal* and fiction co-editor of *Literary Mama*.

Ray Keifetz wrote his first short story at the age of fifteen in a high school English class. He was asked to write a paragraph on what scared him. He handed in a blank sheet of paper, went home, and stayed up all night writing twelve pages about a snow leopard and what scared it. The teacher praised the story but failed him on the assignment. And that pretty much sums up his writing career ever since. Along the way, his poems and stories have appeared in numerous literary journals, including *The Bitter Oleander, Other Voices, Kestrel, Sugar House Review,* and *Burntdistrict*, and he has received a Pushcart Prize nomination. To support his writing—and himself—he has pursued various and sundry occupations, at the moment building furniture and peddling wine. "Miriam's Lantern" was first published by *Clackamas Literary Review* and is part of a recently completed collection of stories entitled *The Hidden Cost of Gifts*.

Diane Lefer has been an animal behavior observer for the research department of the Los Angeles Zoo since 1997. "Alas, Falada!" first appeared in *Faultline* and was included in her collection, *California Transit*, which received the Mary McCarthy Prize and was published by Sarabande Books. She is grateful to the world of independent publishing and salutes small presses, including Ashland Creek, along with those that embraced three of her novels that went homeless for way too long: *Nobody Wakes Up Pretty* (Rainstorm Press, 2012), *The Fiery Alphabet* (Loose Leaves Publishing, 2013), and *The Still Point* (Aqueous Books, scheduled for fall 2014). She volunteers at the Amanda Foundation, offering affection and playtime to the rescue cats and hopes that these sweet creatures, too, soon find homes.

Educated at Harvard and Johns Hopkins, **Rosalie Loewen** lived and worked in a number of countries before settling in rural Alaska with her husband and their two small daughters. She spends her free time outdoors seeking inspiration from the natural world while keeping a sharp lookout for the neighborhood bears.

Kelly Magee's first collection of stories, *Body Language* (University of North Texas Press), won the Katherine Ann Porter Prize for Short Fiction. Her writing has appeared in *The Kenyon Review, The Tampa Review, Diagram, Ninth Letter, Black Warrior Review, Colorado Review*, and others. She is an assistant professor of creative writing at Western Washington University.

Charlotte Stephanie Malerich works and writes near the District of Columbia. "Meat" first appeared in *The Again* No. 11 in 2013. Other short stories have appeared online in *Aphelion*, as well as Sorcerous Signals and its print counterpart *Mystic Signals*. Her current projects include an urban fantasy novel and a graphic novel version of her short story "The 12th Fairy." She lives with one human and two rescued rabbits. Go vegan, stay vegan.

Midge Raymond's short-story collection, *Forgetting English,* received the Spokane Prize for Short Fiction and "lights up the poetry-circuits of the brain" (*Seattle Times*). Originally published by Eastern Washington University Press in 2009, the book was reissued in an expanded edition by Press 53 in 2011. Her work has appeared in the *Los Angeles Times* magazine, *TriQuarterly, American Literary Review, Bellevue Literary Review, Witness,* and other publications.

Jean Ryan, a native Vermonter, lives in Napa, California. A horticultural enthusiast and chef of many years, Jean's writing has always been her favorite pursuit. Her stories and essays have appeared in a variety of journals, including *Other Voices, Pleiades, The Summerset Review, The Massachusetts Review, The Blue Lake Review, Damselfly*, and *Earthspeak*. Nominated twice for a Pushcart Prize, she has also published a novel, *Lost Sister*. Her debut collection of short stories, *Survival Skills*, was published in April 2013 by Ashland Creek Press. Please visit her website at http://jean-ryan.com.

The daughter of a veterinarian, **Jessica Zbeida** grew up in the company of animals. During her education, Jessica worked with a variety of writers, including Zulfikar Ghose, Frederick and Steven Barthelme, Mary Robison, John Tait, and Barbara Rodman. She spends her time teaching, writing, reading, and bicycling. She lives in North Texas with her husband and four cats.

Acknowledgments

"Alas, Falada!" by Diane Lefer appeared first in *Faultline Journal of Arts and Letters* and was included in the collection *California Transit*, published by and used by permission of Sarabande Books.

"Greyhound" by Jean Ryan previously appeared in *Pleiades* (Winter 1999) and *Eunoia Review* (December 2012) and also appears in her short story collection, *Survival Skills.*

"Aren't You Pretty?" by Patrick Hicks first appeared in *The Big Muddy* as "Burn Unit."

"The Ecstatic Cry" by Midge Raymond first appeared in *Ontario Review* and also appears in her short story collection, *Forgetting English.*

"Pelicans" by Julian Hoffman first appeared in an earlier version in *Terrain.org: A Journal of the Built + Natural Environments.*

"Blue Murder" by Suzanne Kamata was originally published in slightly different form in *Snowy Egret* and *Asia Literary Review.*

An earlier version of "Miriam's Lantern" by Ray Keifetz first appeared in *Clackamas Literary Review.*